Timekeepers:

A Revolutionary Tale

J. Y. Harris

ISBN:1469933314
ISBN-13:9781469933313

LCCN

PROLOGUE

Philadelphia, 1777

The dull murmur of voices could vaguely be heard as they drifted up from the floor below. The woman eased herself out of bed, careful not to disturb her sleeping husband. It was a wonder she could hear anything over his cacophonous snoring, but after living with the man for twenty years she'd learned to ignore the noise.

Her soft-soled slippers were silent on the hardwood floor. She eased the door open and moved quietly down the hall. At the top of the stairs she paused, and determined that the voices were coming from her kitchen. All the better, as these stairs did not lead to that room, but to the front of the house.

She slipped down the final steps to the ground floor, and padded quickly toward the door leading to the kitchen, whence the voices came. There was a linen closet next to the doorway, where she kept her tablecloths and other household fabrics. Quietly she opened the closet door, and folded herself under the shelf, carefully closing the door as best she could.

The darkness in the small, confined space didn't bother her; instead, she reached up until she felt the edge of the small hinged door. The access door was built to be opened from the adjoining kitchen, for easy access to cleaning cloths and such, although it was rarely used; in fact, from the kitchen the small door was somewhat hidden behind clusters of dried herbs hanging on the wall.

With the small door ajar, even only an inch, the voices from the kitchen were much clearer, the words easy to discern. She listened, hardly daring to breathe. Ten, fifteen, twenty minutes—she didn't know how much time had passed. Her toes began to tingle as her cramped position cut off their circulation; if she wasn't careful she'd have trouble walking when the time came to leave. By now, however, she'd heard enough.

Pushing the closet door open carefully, she gingerly set a foot flat onto the floor. At first there was no feeling there, but her leg held the weight. Exiting the closet completely, she eased the door closed behind her and quickly made her way back to the stairs. She flew up the steps, instinctively avoiding the places where they creaked. Padding back along the hall to her bed chamber, the woman slipped back into the room and quietly closed the door behind her. She took a few deep breaths to try to steady her breathing and climbed gingerly back under the thick, plain quilt.

With the coverlet pulled under her chin, she turned her face from the door. Her husband barely stirred, and his snoring continued uninterrupted.

Good thing, too, she thought. Not twenty seconds after the woman settled herself in the bed, the door of the bed chamber opened—quietly, yet still audible to her alert ears. Through one open eye she saw shadows dance on the opposite wall as a candle was held aloft from the doorway. Her breathing now returned to a regular rhythm, she waited for the light to be withdrawn and the door to close.

With a sigh, she listened as footsteps receded down the hallway. She had no idea what time it was, but the hour didn't matter—she wouldn't sleep much in any case. She had to come up with a plan, which had to be put in motion as soon as the sun came up.   There was less than 48 hours to avert disaster.

CHAPTER ONE

"How did I let you talk me into this?" Kristen muttered as she made her way across the paved parking lot. She wasn't used to wearing such cumbersome clothes; even in late autumn they were hot and uncomfortable. "It's Saturday morning. I should be at home--asleep."

"For one thing," her brother Brad replied, adjusting his messenger bag on his shoulder, "this, including the essay, is an automatic credit toward our community service requirement for graduation. Something which you should take seriously, considering your study habits and GPA. Someone from the Service Committee is going to be watching to be sure you're actively taking part and not just sitting around like a lump in period costume."

His tone implied that that was exactly what he suspected Kristen would be doing.

Kris grunted. "Why didn't I just volunteer to sort canned goods at the food bank? In the afternoon?"

"I've got two words to answer that one," Brad answered. "Eric Tyson. Once I told you he was going to be here, you practically begged to come along."

She paused, automatically smoothing the long, heavy layers of skirts around her. Ahh... Eric Tyson. Yep, he was a pretty good incentive. If she absolutely had to be out early on a chilly Saturday morning, dressed like a teenaged Betsy Ross in an eighteenth-century-style dress, Eric was a good reason to do it.

But, no need to actually concede the point to her brother.

"Hmmph," she said. "I still can't figure out why the two of you are friends. I mean, after all, he's cool."

Brad didn't rise to the bait. "Oh, come on. Eric and I have known each other since third grade."

She gave an unladylike snort. "But you were never particularly good friends."

"So? Now we're in the same Physics class. And English."

They had left the pavement of the parking lot behind and followed a well-travelled path into the wooded area. A Parks and Recreation department sign at the edge of the parking lot marked it as the way to the "Revolutionary War Site - Battle of White Marsh." As they walked down the uneven dirt trail, Kristen was glad she had thought to wear her sturdy Pumas under the heavy colonial-style skirt, instead of her canvas Keds.

"But he's captain of the baseball team," she said, going back to their conversation about Eric.

"Yeah, I'm aware of that, since I'm on the team too."

"Please. You play outfield."

"So what? This isn't T-ball, when the kids who don't pay attention are put in right field because nobody ever hits the ball there."

"If you say so."

"Come on, Carlos Beltran is an outfielder, and Ichiro Suzuki—I know you've heard of him. Plus, you know that guy whose poster on my wall that you like to look at, Hunter Pence? Outfielder."

Kristen waved her hand in submission. "Okay, whatever. So you and Eric are on the same team, in some classes together, best friends and all that. That doesn't tell me why a cool guy like him is doing this particular activity."

"Um, maybe because he's interested in history? He's the one who brought up this Revolutionary War battle re-enactment in class, and got it included in the community service list. I think he mentioned that his family lived here back then. Anyway, how often can you see Eric Tyson in buckskin breeches, carrying a musket and powderhorn?"

Kristen was silent for a moment as she contemplated the image. "You're right, who am I to question motive?"

"Speaking of motive, I just think it'll be cool to see how those guys fought battles back then. You know: no radar, no automatic weapons, no stealth bombers."

"No running water, no cell phones, no electricity." Kris adjusted the bodice of her dress for the fifteenth time. The bodice was square-cut, as close to colonial style as she could find in the wardrobe closet of the school's drama department. The dress itself was dark blue, long-sleeved, with a white underskirt attached. Luckily, the length was just about right, so that she wasn't tripping over the skirt, and long enough so that her Puma Easy Riders stayed mostly hidden. However, for someone who was more comfortable in jeans, and in fact hadn't worn a dress—of any length—since she'd attended her cousin's wedding, two years ago, this faux-colonial monstrosity was driving her nuts.

Well, at least she didn't have to wear the "mob cap" that the drama teacher had recommended. For one thing, it was butt-ugly. For the second thing, if Kristen's memory served, those caps were only worn indoors, while doing household chores, and not outside. Thirdly, she didn't *want* to have that moldy old cap covering her hair. Kristen Everheart knew she was no beauty—'cute,' maybe, yes, but 'beautiful,' not so much—but one thing she was proud of was her hair. It was a rich chestnut brown, long and a little wavy, with auburn highlights that shone in the sun.

No way she was going to cover it with that mob cap.

Timekeepers: A Revolutionary Tale

"What's in the backpack?" Brad asked, nodding toward the burden on her shoulder. "I know what I've got in my messenger bag, since I tend to actually think ahead and prepare for things, but what do *you* have? Don't tell me you actually brought school work with you?"

Kristen snorted. "Yeah, right! This is stuff I had when I slept over at Abby's last weekend—magazines, PSP, stuff like that to pass the time. I just grabbed it on my way out in case we have to hang around and do nothing for a while." With luck, she had a spare sweatshirt and jeans in there as well, so that she could get out of this revolutionary-era get-up as soon as possible when they were done.

She almost ran into Brad as she realized he had stopped in his tracks. And thank heaven he wasn't wearing one of those ridiculous tricorn hats; otherwise, she'd have gotten one right in the eye.

"Wait a minute," he said just as she was about to make a smart remark. "I've lost my bearings. Did we get off the trail?"

"I don't see how. We've been on it a thousand times, and it's a wide, well-worn—hmmm. Well, apparently it's not as worn as it used to be. Where did it go? And what's with this fog? That came in quickly."

"I know," Brad replied. "This is weird. I just can't tell which way to go to the battle site."

"Let's backtrack to the parking lot and start again," Kristen suggested, hitching up her backpack to turn around.

"Won't work," her brother said. "The path is no clearer behind us than it is in front of us. Or in any other direction."

"That can't be. We couldn't have wandered *that* far off the trail; one of us would've noticed."

"Yeah, you'd think. But wait." Brad fished in his messenger bag. The bag was olive green, sort of the color of military fatigues; it wasn't the best match with his rustic-looking outfit, which was mainly brown and blue, but otherwise the canvas bag could almost pass as a colonial-era item.

He continued. "One of the many advantages to having a smart phone—which I paid for myself, by the way, and didn't have to pester mom and dad to buy for me—but one of the advantages of it is having GPS capability. I'll just check the map to see where we are and where we're going."

Good thinking, Kristen thought, although she didn't say it out loud. No need to give her brainy brother more of a swelled head than he already had.

"All right, here we go, and…. Okay, that's odd. It's not working. I can't get a GPS fix."

"Try calling Eric and see where he is. Maybe he's having the same trouble we are."

Brad found Eric's number and hit 'dial.' "Nothing. It's not connecting. In fact, I'm not getting any service here."

Kristen checked her own phone. "Yeah, me either—no bars. Maybe the fog is interfering somehow?"

"I don't see how. There's a cell tower just across from the park entrance. I used my phone when I was here skateboarding a few weeks ago, and it was really overcast that day, so I don't think a little fog should interfere."

"Well, I'm not sure I'd call this a 'little fog.' This isn't like any fog I've ever seen."

"Yeah, me either. In any case, we can't just stand here all day until this super-fog burns off. We should probably pick a direction and make our way as best we can."

"Good idea. Eventually we'll have to run into something we recognize. So, pick a direction." Kristen had to admit—to herself, at least—that she was a little spooked. The fog was really disorienting. She didn't care at the moment about tweaking her nerd-boy older brother or getting the best of him; there was plenty of time for that once they were at the re-enactment site. Right now she just wanted to be somewhere familiar, with other people.

And out of this blasted cloud of nothingness.

"Alright," Brad said. "Let's continue in the direction we were originally heading. Or as close as we can determine, anyway."

He and Kristen grabbed their bags and made their way forward.

They must have really gotten off the trail, Kris thought. There *was* a path, but it was nothing like the wide, well-trod park trail that they'd been on previously. This one was barely noticeable, just a small track in the undergrowth. She didn't remember seeing any trails in the park that looked like this one. At least, no *official* trails.

And still the fog. Brad was lucky he could see a foot in front of him.

"If I'm not mistaken," he said, as if he'd heard her thoughts, "and if we're going anywhere close to the right direction, we should be coming up on the kids' playground just up ahead. Then the re-enactment site is a little past that."

"I remember that playground. It had those cool little digging toys, like a back-hoe and an excavator. Remember? I used to sit on one of those and pretend I'd built the whole playground and cleared the trees out in that triangle shape."

"Triangle shape?"

"Yeah, don't you remember? The playground was sort of a triangle. The slides were at one corner, the swings in another, and that climbing place—the jungle gym, or whatever—was in the other corner."

"That's right, I remember now. And the 'climbing place,' as you call it, was a pirate ship. And I was an awesome pirate, climbing and swooping all over that thing. Aha!" Brad said. "I think we're coming up on the playground now. The fog is lifting, at any rate."

It was true; Kris could see farther into the woods now than she could have a few minutes ago. And there was a clearing up ahead. Thank god!

"Oh, no. What the--?"

Kristen followed her bother out of the woods as the last of the fog cleared. "You're kidding!"

It was a clearing, all right, but definitely not the playground. Instead, the clearing offered nothing but overgrown grass and weeds.

"Crap!" Brad said. "We couldn't have been so far off course that we missed it entirely. I wish I had a park map; I don't even remember there being a clearing like this with nothing in it."

"Me either. And listen... shouldn't we be able to hear something? Traffic from the highway, or something?"

"Maybe, maybe not, but—" Brad looked all around. "Uh-oh...."

"Uh-oh, what? What's uh-oh? Don't try to spook me; I'm not in the mood."

"I'm not trying to spook you. But, for real, look around the clearing. What do you notice?"

"What do I notice? I notice a clearing, surrounded by a bunch of trees. And filled with weeds and small brush. And probably some rabbits or other critters skittering around that I really don't want to know about." Kris pretended to ignore the tall grass nearby that was moving as something passed by; she looked at her brother instead. "Why? What am I supposed to see?"

Brad pointed. "Can't you just 'see' some slides over in that corner, and some swings over there, and an awesome pirate ship you can climb on over there?"

Kris looked around. "What? Are you trying to tell me...? What *are* you trying to tell me?"

"This is a triangle. See the three angles? Just like the playground."

"So?"

"So, where's the playground? And what happened to the trail? We both know we didn't get off that trail."

"Brad, what are you trying to say, that we're in some sort of alternate reality in which the park isn't the park?"

"I don't know. I have no idea what's going on. But the trail that disappeared, and that fog, and now this…."

"Come on, you're nuts. We just got lost, that's all. It's not like we stumbled into *The Land Before Time*."

"Well, we stumbled into something."

"Yeah, I'll believe that when dinosaurs step out of the woods. Now let's keep going. I don't like just standing here in the middle of nowhere. Especially with who-knows-what crawling around in this tall grass."

Her brother grunted. "You're just as spooked as I am, and you know it."

"So? I'm not gonna get *un*spooked just by standing here."

"I know, I know. Let's see—"

He was interrupted by a shout, which came from somewhere in the trees on the far side of the triangle.

"Well, hallelujah," Kris said. "That sounded human enough. With luck, that's our group of re-enactors and this whole thing—" she gestured to indicate the triangular clearing— "is just some bizarre coincidence. Let's go."

They set off again through the overgrown clearing, Kristen's dress dragging through the high weeds. Brad at least was wearing eighteenth-century-style breeches which weren't as bulky or heavy as her dress. The drama department's costume closet had been a little more generous to guys than it was to girls; there had been a good supply of below-the-knee pants—oops, make that breeches—from which to choose. Coats, too. Brad was wearing a dull, dark cranberry coat with matching vest. Underneath he wore a shapeless, white long-sleeved shirt that was so long, he practically had to tuck it into his pant-legs. Add to that the white calf-covering stockings and some black shoes, and he was geared up pretty convincingly.

As the two teens entered the woods on the far side of the triangle, the sound of voices became louder. They also could smell wood-smoke, and hear the sound of activity and an occasional burst of laughter. Finally, when they were about thirty yards into the woods, Brad and Kris could see where the sounds and voices were coming from. They stopped to survey the scene.

The trees ended not far ahead, and beyond that was a large flat field. On the near side of the field were some Revolution-era canvas tents and two campfires. Men milled around, some sitting around the fire drinking from tin cups, others cleaning weapons. In short, it looked like every Revolutionary War campground re-enactment that Brad or Kristen Everheart had ever seen.

Running along the camp was a road—well, a track, really, not much more than about four or five feet wide—that lead into the woods off to the side.

"Finally," she said. "I need to sit down. And maybe there's better cell reception here than there was back there in the woods."

She started to head toward the encampment, but Brad grabbed her arm.

"Wait. Something's wrong."

"What do you mean?" Kris shook off her brother's hand. "Look, it's early on a Saturday morning, and we just got lost in woods we've been traipsing through our whole lives. And now we found civilization—well, so to speak. What could be wrong?"

"But I don't think that *is* civilization."

Kristen gave an exasperated sigh. "Again: what are you talking about?"

He gestured to the scene ahead. "What is wrong with that picture?"

"What? Nothing!"

"I don't recognize any of those guys, do you?"

Kristen looked through the trees at the men. "Well, no. They're probably just re-enactors from town."

"Most of whom we know. Where's Mr. Elliott from the hardware store? Or that guy, Hamilton, who works at the library? And you *know* Leonard Sidlow would be there, front and center."

Kristen looked again. Brad was right—she didn't recognize any of those men, not from town and not from other re-enactments she'd seen. Even Loony Leonard Sidlow, Nerd Supreme at White Marsh High School. He would definitely be there.

"Well," she said hesitantly, "could they be re-enactors from some other town? Maybe our guys are camped somewhere else."

"Possible, but I doubt it. Look at them: they look tired, disheveled, unshaven. I mean, I know re-enactors grow beards or let their hair get long sometimes, in order to look historically accurate, but…" Brad shook his head. "These guys don't look like they just quit shaving for the past week for this event. Hey, look, speak of the devil."

He pointed to where one soldier was sitting on a large rock, and another one used a pair of large, ancient-looking scissors to trim the man's hair.

"Wow," Kristen said, "that guy must be desperate for a haircut. Somehow I don't think the dude with the scissors works at the Yankee Clipper for his day job."

Brad apparently wasn't listening. "Look at their uniforms," he muttered. "Look how old and dirty and mismatched they are."

"Yeah, that's not unusual, right? It's supposed to be seventeen-seventy-seven. The Continental Army didn't have a single standard uniform, especially this early in the war. You know that. You know more about this stuff than I do."

"You're right, I do," he said, "but look at them. What kind of re-enactor would let his uniform get all dirty and torn like that? Serious re-enactors either pay good money for their uniform, or make it themselves. And I know these uniforms are supposed to look worn and distressed, but a good re-enactor would never let his uniform look like these do."

Kris shifted uneasily where she stood, not liking what she was hearing. "So, what are you saying? That these are some sort of uber-re-enactors who don't believe in showering or folding their clothes?"

Brad took a breath. "No…. I don't think these are re-enactors—at all."

CHAPTER TWO

"Not re-enactors? What are you talking about? What else would they be?"

Brad had that intense look he got when he was thinking. "Call me crazy, but… I think this is the real thing."

"The real thing as in, professional re-enactors?"

"No, the real thing as in the real thing. Those guys don't look like they're re-enacting the Revolution. They look like they're *fighting* it."

"Fighting the Revolution. You mean real eighteenth-century soldiers. Redcoats and muskets and Valley Forge and all that. That's what you think."

Brad looked at his sister, and Kris was a little afraid not to see a hint of teasing in his face. A few weeks ago he'd had her almost convinced that Chace Crawford was going to be stopping at a nearby mall while he was in Philadelphia for a publicity shoot. But at the last minute Kristen had seen the amused glint in Brad's eye and knew he was baiting her. She hadn't spoken to him for a week.

But she didn't see that look now.

"What, are you serious?" she said, her voice rising. "That's not possible."

"That's what I would have thought fifteen minutes ago. But since then we've had a weird fog, a trail that literally disappeared under our feet, a missing playground, and no cell service. If you've got a better explanation for all that, I'm all ears."

Kristen tried to make sense of things. Everything Brad had said was true. By itself, each occurrence he'd mentioned was strange enough. All together, they were just plain weird. Crazy weird.

"Time travel doesn't exist," she said, but even she knew she was trying to convince herself as much as argue with her brother. "You know more about science than I do, but come on, this whole *Back to the Future* stuff—it's not possible. Is it?"

He shook his head. "Like I said, fifteen minutes ago I wouldn't have thought so."

Kristen shrugged. "So, what do we do now? Regardless of what century we're in, we're still stuck in the woods. We can't just stand here for two hundred and thirty years, or… whatever. We've got to do *something*."

"You're right. We need to find out what's going on, one way or another. Maybe I'm wrong and this is all one huge set of strange coincidences. But either way, we need a game plan to—." He stopped suddenly and put up a hand. "Do you hear that?" he whispered. "I think I hear something."

Kristen heard it too: a rustling in the woods from someplace behind them. It was too loud to be a rabbit or a squirrel, and even a deer would have been quieter.

"I see something!" she replied in a whisper of her own. "Over there, heading toward the soldiers' clearing. Somebody wearing a cloak, I think."

It was hard to see through the trees. Even though it was autumn and a lot of the leaves had fallen, the woods were still pretty dense.

"It's not a man's cloak. That's a girl—or a woman. Well, maybe it's time to find out where we are. And when."

She grabbed Brad's arm as he started to move. "Where are you going?" she demanded.

"Look, you just said we have to do something. So, I'm doing something."

"Yeah, I just hope it's not something stupid," she muttered.

Kristen followed her brother through the woods as he moved to intercept the woman. It was hard to walk quietly among the trees and on all the leaves that had fallen, so she and Brad didn't even bother to try. As a result, Kris could tell that the other person heard them, and stopped to see who was approaching.

As the siblings got closer, they could see the person was indeed a woman, but she was a young woman, probably close to their own age. She was of average height, with brown eyes and long light-brown hair which could stand a good brushing, and a bonnet whose strings were tied around her neck hung loosely down her back in a way that Kristen had seen on reruns of "Little House on the Prairie." The young woman had obviously been travelling a good distance, as her cheeks were pink from the exertion; also, the bottom of her green dress was dirty and her brown cloak had burrs and leaves stuck to it.

However, what really dismayed Kristen—and scared her, too, frankly—was the girl's shoes. They were heavy, boxy, and supremely uncomfortable-looking. Kris had heard that in the eighteenth century, shoes were not made for the right or left foot; they were both shaped the same. Interchangeable. They were very clunky-looking. No twenty-first century girl, re-enactor or not, would be caught dead with a pair of these so-called shoes on her feet.

"Good day," the girl said, smiling uncertainly at these two strangers—no doubt crazy-looking—who'd come rushing through the woods to stand before her.

Brad didn't say anything. Kristen thought she heard some "ers" and "hmms" come out of him, but so far, nothing useful.

For someone who was trying to find out what's going on, he was going about it awfully strangely.

"Hi," Kris said, since one of them had to say something intelligent. "We're very glad to see you. We're glad to see anyone."

By now her brother seemed to have found his voice. "Yes, this is a fortuitous meeting."

Kristen had to keep her jaw from dropping. *'Fortuitous'? Who uses the word 'fortuitous'? Who under the age of fifty, that is.*

Brad didn't seem to notice his sister's look as he continued. "We're wondering if you can help us. Answer a question or two. We seem to—er, that is, we seem to have become—"

"We're lost," Kristen blurted out. This time Brad did glare at her in exasperation. "What?" she retorted to him. "We are."

After another irritated look, Brad continued. "Yes, actually we have become disoriented and could use some direction."

The girl smiled again. "Perhaps I can help," she said. "Whither are you bound?"

'Whither are we bound?' Kristen thought to herself. *Good question. Should we take that literally, and tell her where we were heading, physically, in terms of actual real estate? Or maybe we should correct the girl's question and instead try to tell her* when *we were headed; that is, what year we want to end up in?*

"Well," Brad said to the young woman, obviously thinking quickly, "we're trying to get to—er—Flourtown."

Now it was Kristen's turn to stare at her brother. Flourtown? Really? Why would they want to go there? Especially in these blasted colonial get-ups.

"I'm headed in that general direction myself, to the mill," the girl said, showing them some empty burlap-looking sacks she'd been holding—as if that was supposed to mean something to Kristen and Brad. "If you'd like, I see no reason why we can't all walk together."

She continued in the direction she'd been heading, and the Everhearts fell into step with her. "By the way, my name is Rebecca. Rebecca Darrow. May I know your names as well, since we may be travelling together?"

"Uh, yeah, sure. I'm Brad Everheart and this is my sister Kristen."

"Nice to meet you," Rebecca replied, "although…."

"What is it?" Brad asked. "Is something wrong?"

"N-no. No, I'm sure there's not. It's just—I've never seen sacks or bags like those that you wear. Such strange material. And with words and designs on them!"

Uh-oh, Kristen thought. *She's talking about my backpack and Brad's messenger bag. They're new, they're modern, totally twenty-first century. Straight from the Trailsman Outfitter store. This chick doesn't know what they are; she's never seen anything like them before in her life. Between this and the shoes….*

We're screwed.

"They're, um, they're a new material," Brad said. "We just got them. They're from a place called Franklin Mills Mall."

Rebecca frowned. "I've never heard of it. Is it far from Philadelphia? Or is it in your home country?"

"I *wish* Franklin Mills was my home country," Kristen said before she could stop herself. "But our family is actually from Germany."

"Prussia," Brad corrected her. "It's called Prussia these days, remember?"

Kristen rolled her eyes. "Of course. Whatever was I thinking?"

Rebecca smiled. "My family is from Ireland."

"Yes, I thought I noticed an accent."

"Did you now? You should hear my mother. She and da came over the water after they were wed, so they still speak strongly with the Irish brogue."

Kristen felt like she was in a dream. Actually it was more like a nightmare. She would give anything to see Ashton Kutcher and some camera guys jump out of the woods and yell "Punk'd!"

Not likely, though. With Kris's luck the only ones jumping out of the woods would be natives, with tomahawks drawn.

"Why are you walking through the woods?" Brad asked. "We saw some soldiers in a clearing back there—"

"No," Rebecca interrupted. "I'm staying away from the encampments. At least until I reach Green Valley."

"Wait, I thought you were going to Flourtown?"

"I am," Rebecca replied. "But Green Valley is on the way."

"No, it's not," Brad insisted. "Green Valley isn't all that far from Flourtown, but it's not on the way."

Rebecca stopped. "For someone who's lost, you certainly seem to know where things are."

"My brother knows all sorts of trivia," Kristen broke in. "Batting averages, football statistics, physics equations—you name it, and if it's useless and geeky, he knows it."

The other girl looked at Kristen quizzically. "I don't know any of those things you mention; I don't even know what they are. But as I said, you do seem to know a lot about what's nearby for someone who claims to be lost."

"Don't worry," Brad replied. "I just like to look at maps, which is how I know about Green Valley. But right now I think you're the one who knows more than either one of us."

They walked a little further and Brad spoke again. "So why are you staying away from encampments?"

"Because I'm in a hurry. Most of the time when you come across soldiers, they want to talk and ask what news you have, what's the latest from Philadelphia, is there any word from New York or elsewhere. I don't have time for idle conversation. My mother charged me with a task, and I must hurry."

"Yeah, gotta get that flour. Heaven forbid the pies and biscuits don't get made on time," Kristen muttered. "Don't want to jeopardize the whole colonial infrastructure with some tardy baked goods."

Brad shot her a dirty look, which Kristen ignored.

"So, is there a reason you're walking through the woods, instead of, say—oh, I don't know, on a nice, flat road?"

Rebecca turned and smiled at Kristen. "I admit it may seem strange, but it's actually quicker this way. It's a more direct route, and I don't have to worry about stopping at each patrol checkpoint. Even though I have a pass, it's still easier to avoid them."

Brad and Kristen looked at each other. "A pass?" Brad repeated. "What kind of pass?"

Rebecca looked at them, her brow furrowed. "The kind of pass that gets me through the patrols. Don't you have a pass? The royal army won't let anyone travel outside of Philadelphia without one."

Brad smiled. Kristen knew that smile. It was the one he used when he was trying to talk his way into something: a movie on a school night; borrowing the car; pretending 'War Quest America' is rated for ages fourteen and up, instead of eighteen and up.

In this case, Brad was trying to talk his way *out* of something. "Actually, we don't have a pass," he said. When Rebecca looked at him in alarm, he continued. "We didn't come from Philadelphia. We came from—er, Falls Village."

Their companion looked at them uncertainly. "Aren't there soldiers there as well? I understood the British held all of Philadelphia and the surrounding area."

"Yes, the British are there, but there are no officers issuing passes. It's just a small outpost... it's not a city like

Philadelphia. The villagers are very scattered into the countryside."

Rebecca still looked skeptical, and Kristen was afraid that Brad was going to try to 'explain' further. *Stop talking*, she thought, trying to send a mental message to her brother. *Don't oversell. Just keep your mouth shut and leave it at that.*

To her surprise he seemed to have read her mind and didn't say anything further.

Kristen thought it was time to change the subject. "So, do you have any family members who are fighting?" Normally she would have used the phrase 'in the military,' but other than its similarity to the word 'militia,' she didn't know if Rebecca would recognize this use of the word. And she certainly couldn't ask about specific branches of the military; they were about a hundred and thirty years too early for the Air Force, the Navy wasn't more than a handful of volunteer ships, and ditto for the Marines. That left only the Army—and what was here was hardly the organized, well-trained, well-equipped fighting force that Kristen had heard about all her life.

Of course, Rebecca Darrow didn't know any of that. "Yes," she answered, "my brother William is with the 2nd Pennsylvania. Right now they're bivouacked nearby."

"Oh? How old is he?"

"Turned eighteen last May."

Wow, Kristen thought, just about a year older than Brad. She tried to imagine Brad going off to war. Of course, boys did that all the time in her time, too, joining one branch of the military or another right out of high school. Girls too, for that matter. It was hardly an uncommon thing. Probably some of her own class members would enlist after graduation.

But if they did, they would sign up, have a few weeks, or even months, before reporting for duty, and then go off to a six- or eight-week training camp to get in shape and get accustomed to the military lifestyle. After that they'd probably get assigned somewhere else for more specific training. Bottom line: as far as Kristen knew, it would be months before any new soldiers got deployed to Iraq, or Afghanistan, or wherever their duty station was to be, whether it's a place where there's 'action' or not.

Unlike Rebecca's brother, who probably decided to join, or was urged to join, and was likely gone a day or two later. And rather than having a uniform issued to him, and being assigned a weapon or other equipment on which he would be trained, William would have taken whatever clothes he had, and his own musket.

And this country, she thought, *my country—or rather, the colonies—is relying on these young, untrained, ill-equipped boys to go up against the British military machine, which was undeniably the world's mightiest army of the day.*

Kristen found it mind-boggling. She knew the facts and the history. She'd heard often enough about the 'rag-tag Continental Army.' But it wasn't until now, today, when she was experiencing it herself, that she could appreciate how risky it had been, and how crazy and unbelievable it really was.

The trio of young people had long ago passed by the encampment that Brad and Kristen had seen earlier. The one near where the 'playground' was. Or would be, in about two hundred and some-odd years.

"Do you have any idea where we are?" Brad asked his sister as he dropped back to walk beside her.

"Yeah. Apparently we're on our way to Flourtown, wherever the heck that is, and for whatever good it'll do us."

"Well, near as I can figure, Flourtown is a few miles north of the park where we started."

"But what are we gonna do when we get there? Nothing there is going to help us get back to our own time, and we don't have one of these almighty passes she keeps talking about."

"I know. And honestly I don't know *what* we'll do when we get there."

"Then why are we going? We're trudging through the woods to someplace we don't have any reason to go."

"Well, we don't have any reason not to, either. Plus, this way we're not wandering around in the woods by ourselves, not knowing where we are. If you've got any other ideas, I'm open to suggestion."

"Since you mention it, may I point out that we're moving *away* from the place that brought us here? Maybe that mystery fog—and the place where the fog was—is the key to getting back. Maybe we should've stayed put."

"And do what? Stand there in the middle of the forest all day? The fog disappeared, remember? It's not like we could have walked back through it to the other side, because it's gone."

Kristen sighed. "I just wonder if we'll ever get back. I mean, what if we're stuck here?"

Brad thought for a second. "Nah, I don't think so. It would bring on a variation of the Grandfather Paradox."

"What's that?"

"It's a theoretical situation in which someone goes back in time and changes some detail which may or may not seem important, but could change the future—his own future. For example, if you went back a hundred years and somehow caused your own grandfather to die before he fathers any children. In that case, your father or mother would never be born, and therefore *you* would never exist. That's the paradox: if you never exist, you can't go back in time, and if you go back in time, you might change things to the point you would never exist." He took a breath. "See? You get it now? Who knew, watching sci-fi shows can actually come in handy. They're geeky, but useful."

Kristen just shook her head. "Well, I hope you're right about us not being stuck here. I don't want to miss out on my prom, or getting my driving permit. Not to mention the fact that I absolutely insist on having indoor plumbing and a decent hairdryer."

Timekeepers: A Revolutionary Tale

Rebecca turned to check on the siblings. "Are you two lagging behind for a reason, or are you just slow?"

Kris smiled. "Well, well, the colonial girl has a sense of humor after all. Good to hear. No, we're cool."

"I know. The weather has turned quite chilly in the past week. Autumn is here full force. Now, why are you smiling?"

Brad shook his head. "Never mind, it's not important."

"We're going to get on the road soon for the rest of the way. That should make travelling a little easier." Once again, Rebecca took the lead.

"The road will take us directly to Flourtown?"

"Yes, but I do need to make a stop. As I said, my brother's regiment is nearby, along the way, and I have to get a message to him."

"We'll go with you." Brad winced as his sister smacked his arm, but otherwise he ignored her. As usual.

"That's not necessary. My message is urgent and confidential, and I don't wish to delay you on your way to the mill."

"It's not a problem. We're in no particular hurry." This time Brad anticipated Kristen's action, and caught her hand before she could hit him again. "Besides, we want to be sure you get there safely."

Rebecca smiled. In fact, Kristen noticed that she smiled quite nicely—and right in Brad's direction. *Girl, you do not want to go there*, Kris thought. *Brad is not the guy for you. Wrong place, wrong century. When I say he will leave you, I mean he will* leave you*. With any luck, that is.*

They walked on. And on and on, or so it felt to Kristen. No wonder there weren't too many overweight people in this time period, she thought; they walked so dang much. Not to mention, not a Mickey D's in sight. Or Starbucks or TCBY. She supposed the wealthy families probably had nice carriages, like Kristen had seen in movies. Otherwise, most people walked or rode a horse, and maybe a cart or a wagon.

Just their luck she and Brad had to run into someone who had neither.

Suddenly Rebecca halted and held up her hand. "I think I hear something, and I believe it should be the 2nd Pennsylvania regiment. Let me check; stay here."

Before Brad or Kris could say anything, Rebecca slipped into the woods between the trees. She came back quickly. "This is the regiment," she confirmed. "If you feel you must come, follow me."

CHAPTER THREE

Kristen followed Rebecca while Brad took up the rear. The path—more of a narrow track, really—went gradually uphill and when it leveled off, the Everhearts saw a large flat area filled with tents and soldiers. At least, Kristen supposed they were soldiers; only about half wore discernible uniforms.

The men were engaged in various activities. Just like at the other encampment they'd seen, some men were cleaning weapons, some practicing formations, others were involved in various mundane tasks: chopping wood, mending clothes, fixing wagons or other equipment. Off to one side of the encampment Kristen even saw a few men working with what looked like a deer-skin stretched between two poles. She winced and looked away.

Farther off, in a large field behind the tents, were more soldiers. A *lot* more soldiers, numbering in the hundreds, she guessed, apparently engaged in military exercises and drilling.

"Here comes William," Rebecca said.

Kris and Brad watched as a young soldier came to meet them, and gave Rebecca a brotherly hug. "What are you doing here?" he asked, and glanced questioningly at two strangers.

"These are the Everhearts, who I met on my way here. May I present my brother, William Darrow."   After the introductions were made, Rebecca said, "I have an urgent message from Mother. Confidential."

The Darrows stepped away and spoke quietly for a few minutes. She tried not to look, but it became clear to Kristen that there was some matter of disagreement between them. It was like watching a mime performance: Rebecca talked and seemed to insist; William shook his head and gestured negatively, occasionally pointing to the camp over his shoulder. Whatever it was that Rebecca wanted, William wouldn't—or couldn't—comply.

"Now there's a familiar scene," Brad said. "A brother and sister arguing."

"Yeah, who knew that wuss-head brothers exist in every timeline."

"Or stubborn sisters who think the world owes them whatever they want."

Any retort Kristen would have made was cut off as Rebecca and William came to join them. Neither looked happy.

"We have a problem," Rebecca said. "I can't go with you to the mill. My plans have changed and I need to go—er, someplace else."

"What about your 'urgent' mission to buy flour?" Kristen asked. "Those pies aren't going to bake themselves."

Brad gave her one of his usual 'wrinkled brow' looks. It was standard practice and a common occurrence, signifying irritation, annoyance, or just a 'get real!' message.

"Is there anything we can do?" he asked. "We're not in a rush to get to Flourtown, so if we can help in any way…."

Now Kristen gave Brad her own version of the WB—wrinkled brow. Instead of getting them back home where they belong, her brother seemed more interested in chatting up Colonial Cathy.

They had a problem, she and Brad. They were lost in the woods, not to mention lost in time. They had no idea how they got here, or how they'd get back. *If* they'd get back. Worse,

Kristen was soon going to get the full effect of that double glass of OJ she'd had this morning. She did not care to think about what she'd have to do about *that*.

Rebecca and William gave each other meaningful looks, his insistent, hers reproachful, and finally she said, "Very well, I accept your offer to accompany me on my errand. But only reluctantly."

She and her brother said their farewells, and as William returned to his troopmates, Rebecca led the others back to the road.

Brad fell in step beside her. "Don't worry," he said, hoping to reassure her, "there's safety in numbers."

"I'm not worried for my safety," she said. "I'm more concerned about yours."

"Ours? Why should we be in danger?"

"Forgive me, I shouldn't have said anything. We'll be walking together so we should just enjoy pleasant conversation."

They were all silent for a moment, each lost in private thought. Well, so much for 'pleasant conversation.'

"You know," Brad began, "we don't know that much about you."

"That's not quite true," Rebecca answered. "You know considerably more about me than I do about you. You know my name, that I live in Philadelphia, I have a brother named William, and my parents are from Ireland. Also, I'm on my way to get flour. Or, I *was* on my way to get flour."

"And the pies," Kristen chimed in. "Don't forget the pies. Her family likes to bake."

Rebecca looked at her strangely. A look, by the way, that Kristen was all too familiar with, although mainly she was used to it from her brother.

Seeing that look, Brad gave a small snort of amusement. As if to say *I'm glad to know I'm not the only one who thinks Kristen is an annoying nutcase.* "Anyway," he said, "why don't you tell us where we're headed? Surely that can't be much of a secret, and we're going to find out soon enough."

Rebecca seemed to consider this for a moment. "I suppose you're right about that. Very well. We're going to a place called Tyson's Tavern."

Brad and Kristen exchanged looks. "Tyson's Tavern," he repeated.

"Yes. Do you know it?"

"No. That is, we've never been there, but we're—er—acquainted with a member of the Tyson family. At least, I assume it's the same family."

"From back home," Kristen clarified. "Not from here."

"Well, I'm only going there to deliver a message," Rebecca said. "To one of the officers who are there."

"To your brother's commanding officer, you mean," Brad said, stopping in the middle of the dirt road. "You're taking your urgent message to the commander of the 2nd Pennsylvania."

"Yes," Rebecca replied cautiously; obviously she thought he was a nutcase himself. "That much has been obvious so far."

"Yeah," Kristen agreed. "So?"

"So… in reality, the message is actually intended to go to the commander of all the troops in the area, to General Washington himself. I know who you are now," Brad continued, a note of excitement creeping into his voice, "and I know why you're here. Your mother's name is Lydia, and the British have been using your home in Philadelphia as a sort of meeting house, because General Howe and his officers are using the homes nearby as a headquarters. And now you have information for General Washington. Information that your mother overheard from the British."

Rebecca looked frightened. "Who are you? Loyalists? How do you know such things?"

Brad put his hands out in a gesture of calm to reassure her. "No, we're not spies, and we're certainly not Loyalists.

Timekeepers: A Revolutionary Tale

Believe me, we want the Americans to win this war just as much as you do. Or as much as most people, anyway. I know you're Quakers, so I don't know what that means in regard to your thoughts about the war."

Rebecca was obviously still spooked, but she turned and continued walking quickly, as if by doing so she could leave this turn of events behind her.

Kristen was gaping at her brother as if he'd sprouted wings and turned purple. "What the crap are you talking about?" she hissed at him. "Seriously, what gives? Did that fog make you psychic? Or just plain psycho?"

"No, it didn't make me psychic. Although, how cool would that be? All right, listen: you obviously know all about our local connection to the Revolution—the one we're supposed to be re-enacting today. Well, you might not know all the details about how this Battle of White Marsh came about."

Kristen shook her head, and Brad continued.

"When the British army occupied Philadelphia late in seventeen-seventy-seven, General Howe took over some houses for himself and his top officers. Mostly they were houses of Loyalists who were glad to have them, but there were—are—obviously a number of Quakers in town who were pretty neutral on the whole Revolution thing. Anyway, Howe took over one house for their official meetings. It was the house of a Quaker woman, Lydia Darragh.

"One night she eavesdropped on a meeting being held in her kitchen, and heard the British talk about a surprise attack on the Americans—er, the Continental army—in two days' time. When the meeting was over, Lydia hurried quietly back upstairs to her bedroom, and pretended to be asleep when one of the British officers checked on her. The next day, she supposedly used a trip to the flour mill to get the information about the attack to Washington's army, so that's why the Americans were prepared for the attack and the battle went our way."

"So you're saying that our friend pie-girl here is at this very moment taking that information to General Washington?"

"Maybe not to him personally, but to someone who can get it to him, yeah."

"She's carrying out the history that leads to the battle we've heard about our whole lives, and which took place practically in our backyard."

"Yes. Do you care to repeat it a few *more* times?"

"Yeah, funny. I just find this amazing. I mean, how do you know this? Why have I never heard about it?"

"Well, I know about it from research I did for a paper on the Philadelphia Campaign of the Revolution last year. And you've never heard about it because you really don't care about this stuff, and you've never bothered to learn about it."

"I know, right? I mean, its history. It's in the past. It's done and can't be changed. I know about the Battle of White Marsh: that it occurred, how many died on each side, and all that, but I didn't know about all this cloak-and-dagger spy drama that led up to it."

"There's a lot of that 'cloak-and-dagger' stuff all around, if you know where to look for it. Now you're actually living it, whether you like it or not. An insider's look, so to speak."

"Wait a minute," Kristen said. "If you knew this story already, why didn't you recognize it right away, when we first met our friend, here?"

"Because in the accounts I read, the woman's name was Darragh—with a '-agh.' I assumed it rhymed with Farrah, or Sahara. Rebecca said her name was Darrow. At least, that's how she pronounces it: like 'sparrow.' For all I know it could be spelled '-agh' but pronounced like '-ow.'

"And besides, nothing I read mentioned anything about a teenaged girl. All accounts indicate that Lydia herself took the message to the Continental army."

"So why do you think the history books say something different? I mean, the name is different, no mention of Rebecca…."

Timekeepers: A Revolutionary Tale

Brad shrugged. "Who knows? The whole Lydia Darragh story isn't that well-known; I really didn't find much info about it—just one or two small paragraphs in a couple of sources—and what I did find said the story could never be confirmed. In any case, it was probably just a matter of a confusion of facts, things getting distorted in the re-telling. Sort of like that game Telephone, when kids whisper a sentence from one person to another; what the last person hears is rarely what the first person actually said."

"Yeah, I remember. We used to play it at family campouts, with all the cousins? That was fun."

"Well, this is not a game. This is the real deal."

"True. But at least we know how it'll turn out."

At that moment Rebecca made a hissing noise and motioned for them to be quiet. She stopped near a large nearby tree. Brad and Kristen caught up to her and stopped, listening.

In the brush they could hear rustling, then the low murmur of voices.

"Who do you think it is?" Brad whispered. "Friendlies?"

Rebecca shook her head. "I'm not sure. William said they had seen British scouts in the area. I'm afraid they may be trying to get an exact location of Continental forces, or find the best route to—"

When she cut herself off, Brad said, "It's okay. We know they're planning a surprise attack on Washington's army."

Rebecca looked suspicious again. "How do you know that?"

"Nobody told me, I swear. I just—er, figured it out."

"Then you must know something that General Washington doesn't."

"You could say that."

"What does 'okay' mean?"

"What?" Brad and Kristen looked at each other. "Er, it means 'fine,' or 'all right,'" he said.

"Yeah, it's a common word from our native land. Germany."

"Prussia."

"Whatever."

Rebecca looked a bit confused and glanced at Kristen. "You say that word a lot, too: 'whatever.'"

Brad smirked. "You have no idea."

"People, people," Kristen said. "Can we focus, please? Are we forgetting our friends in the woods here? The ones who can probably see us plain as day, even as we stand here yapping?"

"Oh, right," her brother replied. "I assume we're in no danger from them, since we're not soldiers, and they're only scouts."

"You're likely correct," Rebecca agreed. "And I do have a pass issued by General Howe's aide, so that should be protection enough to be on the road."

Brad sighed. He and Kristen had no such pass. Although it was possible the two of them might be able to 'piggyback' on Rebecca's, that was certainly not definite. If the pass specified the number of people for which it was valid, it wouldn't help them at all. They would just have to hope they weren't challenged by any redcoats.

"Soooo…" he said, "shall we get on our way to the tavern?"

"Yes," Rebecca agreed. "It's only another few miles. And we can go the rest of the way by the road."

Yippee, another few miles, Kristen thought. *What's another two or three after the ten we've already walked today? Hi, I'm Miss Revolutionary War of Seventeen Seventy-Seven, and I'm walking to Flourtown. No wait, I'm actually going to see my brother at his army camp. Ha ha, and now we're walking to some backwoods ale-house. Walk, walk, walk. Anybody ever herd of a bicycle? How about a carriage? Why couldn't we have been transported through time to Boston, and run into Paul Revere? At least he had a friggin' horse.*

Timekeepers: A Revolutionary Tale

While Kristen was grumbling, Brad was once again making time with Colonial Cathy up ahead. Unbe-friggin'-lievable. He didn't seem to show this much interest in any girls in the twenty-first century, at least not that she'd ever seen or heard, but didn't it just figure that geekboy is gonna crush on the first girl he meets when they're time-travelling. How very Captain Kirk of him.

Not me, Kristen thought. *Nuh-uh. Pie-girl's brother William had not been my type. At. All. So that cheesy-movie scenario in which a brother-sister combo hooks up with another brother-sister combo?*

No way. Not gonna happen. Hooking up with someone in this timeline is not on my *agenda. I'm flying solo in this century. 'Solo is heaven in 'seventy-seven'—that's my motto. And yeah, that's seventeen-seventy-seven. Nineteen-seventy-seven would be weird enough, but nooo, that's not where we are. We're a couple centuries off. Lucky us!*

After what seemed like another year of walking, the trio could see a couple of buildings up ahead, a place that looked like it had chairs, and a cozy fire, maybe even something to eat. It wasn't exactly a Friendly's, or even a Starbucks, but it had to be better than trudging along this road.

The smoke drifting out of the chimney seemed to be a beacon of welcome to travelers, and as they neared, the Everhearts saw that there were actually a couple of buildings: the tavern, and what appeared to be (or rather, what sounded like) a blacksmith shop, as well as the usual small out-buildings. Kristen and Brad had been to Colonial Williamsburg and other historical locations often enough to recognize that sound of ringing steel on the forge when they heard it.

"Rebecca," Brad said, "how do you want to play this?" At her questioning look, he continued, "I'm assuming you don't know William's commanding officer by sight. That is, you wouldn't recognize him without someone pointing him out, and he might not even agree to speak with you."

She shook her head. "All I know is, his name is Captain Howell. He's only been in charge of the regiment for a few months, since the previous officer was captured at the battle of Germantown. Therefore, I'll just go in to the tavern and ask to speak with Captain Howell."

"And you know he's here… how?" Kristen asked.

"William said all the officers in the regiments were called to a meeting here at Tyson's Tavern."

"Yeah, and what about William?" Kristen wondered. "Why didn't he take the message to his captain?"

"He's scheduled to go on duty shortly. His sergeant would not have allowed him to leave camp."

"Even with a message for their captain?"

"Especially with a message for the captain. William said the sergeant would have demanded to know the information, and would have insisted on carrying it himself."

"And that's bad because…?"

"Yeah," Brad said, "doesn't William trust the sergeant to deliver it?"

"Oh, I'm sure the sergeant would deliver the message. The problem is, not only would he take credit for it—which is hardly important in the long run—but for all we know, he would embellish it. To try to make himself seem more important, and further his career. He might even distort the details."

Brad and Kristen looked at each other. "There's that game of Telephone again," Brad muttered. To Rebecca he said, "And I supposed writing it out wouldn't change that. Or be safe, for that matter. Yeah, we know the type of guy this sergeant is.

"So, you're going to go into the Tavern and ask for Captain Howell. Are you okay with doing that? I mean, he's an Army officer you've never met before, and you're a—er, um, well—you're a young lady."

Rebecca smiled, and put her hand on Brad's arm. Kristen was amused to see her brother turn six shades of red. "Don't worry, Mr. Everheart," Rebecca said. "I will be perfectly safe."

As the young people neared the tavern, they could see more activity. A number of horses were tied to the hitching post out front, and a young boy was currying one of them. Next door at the smithy an old man sat outside on a short barrel, whittling; just like a picture from a history book, Kris thought. From inside the smithy came the sound of voices raised to be heard over the din of the smith's hammer.

Rebecca ignored all this—it was all old hat to her; definitely not out of the ordinary—and led them inside Tyson's Tavern. Brad half-expected someone to approach to ask them for ID and proof of age, since that was what he knew what would happen if he tried to get into such an establishment in his own time.

However, nobody challenged the three young people, and they entered the tavern, blinking as their eyes transitioned from the bright autumn sun to the cool dimness of the indoors. Rebecca walked directly to the bar along the far wall.

"We'll be with you in one moment," came a voice from behind.

The three turned, and Rebecca was puzzled to see her companions' reaction. Both Everhearts seemed to freeze in their tracks. Brad's eyes widened, and Kristen's mouth fell open.

"Er, I'm here to see Captain Howell," Rebecca said, distracted as she was by her companions' odd reaction. "I have an urgent message for him."

"Do you, now?" came the reply. The speaker was a young man, probably their own age. He had a towel over his shoulder and two empty mugs in each hand; obviously he was in the middle of cleaning up.

The tavern-owner's son?

Rebecca cleared her throat—loudly—in an effort to break her companions' trance.

"Yes, I do," she continued. "And who might you be?"

"My name is Jacob Tyson. You say you need to speak with Captain Howell? What makes you think he's here?"

"I see horses outside—officers' horses. Yet the taproom is practically empty. He's got to be here somewhere."

"I never said there weren't people here. What makes you think one of them is this Captain Howell?"

Rebecca gave a sigh of exasperation. "See here, I've been walking—*we've* been walking—for miles, and we're tired. I've come from Philadelphia, and I need to—"

"From Philadelphia!"

The exclamation startled all four young people, and they turned toward the new voice, from the doorway that led to the rooms beyond the taproom. A military man stood there, wearing a blue coat with buff facings, a matching buff-colored waistcoat, and brass buttons which had surely been recently polished, as they reflected brightly in the lantern glow augmenting the sunlight penetrating the two thick windows. Shiny black boots—also freshly-polished—fit over the tan breeches.

"You say you are come from Philadelphia," he continued. "For what purpose? What business have you here?"

Rebecca seemed uncertain in the presence of the no-nonsense officer. "Well, er, I'm here to speak with Captain Howell, of the 2nd Pennsylvania. Are you he?"

"No, miss, I am not. I'm Major John Clark, of General Washington's staff. Again, what is your business with Captain Howell?"

For the first time since entering the tavern, Brad spoke. "General Washington's staff? Is he here? Can we meet him?"

Kristen too had been snapped out of her reverie at the entrance of this officious soldier. Even in the face of all the other surprises of the day, she was amused to see Brad practically falling over himself at the mention of Washington. You'd think he was asking to meet Eli Manning or The Decemberists.

Timekeepers: A Revolutionary Tale

"No, you may not meet him," Major Clark replied. "And I will only ask you once more, young madame, what is your business with Captain Howell?"

"I have a message for him. A confidential message," Rebecca replied. She was trying to retain her dignity and confidence in front of the imposing major.

"From whom?"

From none of your business, Kristen wanted to blurt. Why do some people always think they have a right to know everything? Her homeroom teacher was the same way. If a kid got called to the office, or was given a note from another teacher, she thought it was her business to know all about it.

Rebecca stood firm, although she was clearly nervous. "It's not a message 'from' anyone, but it is information that General Washington needs to know. About General Howe."

"And you were going to give this information to Captain Howell?"

"Yes. He's my brother's commanding officer, and I'm sure he can get it to the right person."

"As it happens," the Major stated, "I am the right person. I collect, er, information for General Washington."

"You're a spymaster!" Brad said, and Kris could almost see the lightbulb that appeared over his head. "You operate a spy ring to gather intel for the Continentals."

If ever anyone could be said to 'look thunderous,' it was Major Clark, at this moment. His brows descended into an ominous 'V' formation, and his otherwise handsome features hardened. "You had best watch your tongue, young sir," he said in a low, tight voice. (*Just like Jack Bauer*, Kristen thought.) "Accusations such as that could cost lives." He turned his stern gaze back to Rebecca. "Now, young lady—"

"My mother is Lydia Darrow," she blurted out, much to everyone's surprise—including, apparently, her own.

Major Clark came as close to looking surprised as he likely allowed himself, but covered quickly. "Lydia Darrow! Well, why didn't you say so? Please, come with me." The

Major looked at the tavern-keeper's son. "Tyson, get these young people some refreshment. That is, if they insist on waiting."

Kristen, Brad, and Jacob watched Major Clark usher Rebecca out of the taproom.

"Will she be safe?" Brad asked... somewhat belatedly, Kris thought.

"Certainly," Jacob replied. "Major Clark is a gentleman, and his only concern is for General Washington's army. Your friend is well protected. Please, have a seat, and I'll bring you something to drink."

Jacob Tyson pulled out a chair at one of the tables, and gestured for Kristen to sit. Brad sat next to her. Then young Tyson hurriedly wiped off another table as he made his way behind the bar. After stowing the dirty mugs and towel, he disappeared into the back room.

He returned a moment later with two cups of something he called 'flip.' At his sister's questioning—and skeptical—look, Brad informed her that it was something like eggnog... although the way he said it, Kristen knew there was more to it than that, and that she probably didn't want to know details. She sipped hers gingerly and tried not to make a face. Eggnog was not something she enjoyed to begin with; anything that was 'something like' it was practically doomed to fail.

"Won't you join us?" she asked, eying the mostly-empty taproom. "I think you can probably spare a minute."

Jacob shrugged. "Yes, I suppose I can at that." He sat down and looked from one to the other of the Everhearts. "Are you from around here? I don't believe I know you."

"We're from Prussia," Kristen stated.

"Falls Village," Brad corrected her.

"Dang, almost had it that time," Kristen said. "But our family is originally from Prussia," she explained to Jacob.

He nodded, and Kristen noticed again the resemblance to his modern-day relative. Jacob had blue eyes and dark blond hair that was just thick enough to make a girl's fingers itch to run through it, and just wavy enough to make him look boyish. She thought he sort of looked like Heath Ledger in that old movie *A Knight's Tale*. (Yum!) His grin also made him look boyish, but there was something in his eyes which made her certain that Jacob Tyson didn't miss much. Behind the friendly, casual appearance, Kristen was sure he was sharp as a tack, a "triple-A" personality, as her dad would say: alert, aware, and assessing.

She decided to test this theory.

"How often is General Washington here?" she asked.

"The General just arrived in the area yesterday," he replied with a shrug. "And how long have you known Miss Darrow?"

Aha! Defend and attack. He obviously was not willing to talk about Washington.

"Not long," Brad replied in answer to the question. "We met her on the road, and were more than happy to walk with her and accompany her here."

"And why is that?" Jacob asked. "If you just met her, that is. I understand her family are Quakers. Are you Quakers as well, and neutral about the war?"

"Oh, we are *so* not Quakers," Kristen said. "I personally love music and dancing, thank you very much."

"That's the Amish, genius," Brad retorted under his breath. To Jacob he said, "No, we're not Quakers, and we're not exactly neutral about the war. We're definitely on the side of the Americans. You might say our future depends on it."

"Ha, clever," Kris muttered as she held up her mug, reluctantly, for another sip of flip.

Jacob merely nodded, although it looked to Kristen like he wasn't completely convinced. Ah, well, time to change the subject.

"Soooo. Jacob Tyson. Tyson's Tavern. Conveniently located here, just outside of Philadelphia. How long has your family owned this place?"

"My grandfather opened it, before the war with the Indians. This road was a common route out of Trenton, so the tavern was a convenient stopping point and changing station for horses. How about you, what does your father do in Falls Village? Farmer? Shopkeeper?"

Kristen laughed aloud at the notion of her father being a farmer. Mowing the yard, yeah, dad certainly did that—unless he got Brad to do it instead. But dad didn't even want to get involved in the small kitchen garden their mom started in the back yard; other than maybe setting the sprinkler on it upon request, that is. Basically, if it wasn't for the great beef stew and veggie pizza his wife made from time to time—sometimes with veggies from that very garden—Kevin Everheart wouldn't know an onion from a rutabaga.

"Our dad works with... er, machines," Brad said.

"Dad?" Jacob repeated, as if he were unfamiliar with the word.

"Father," Kristen said. "He means father. 'Dad' is a Prussian word for father." *What the heck*, she thought; *like he'll ever find out otherwise.*

"Oh, I see. And what type of machine does he work with?"

"What type of machine?"

"Yes. Plow, printing press, the spinning jenny or steam engine...."

"Well, I guess you could say he works with a printing press. It definitely prints. But it's a new kind; too complicated for me to explain."

Jacob seemed to accept that answer. Which was good, because if they had to explain 'dad' to him, how would they ever hope to explain what a software engineer did?

Kristen was glad Jacob didn't ask more questions about it, because she really liked looking at him when his brow was clear and his features untroubled. Eric Tyson was a doll in the twenty-first century, and even though there was a definite difference between the two—other than age and century born—she found Jacob Tyson just as good looking as his descendent.

Let Brad spend his time here in 1777 chatting up the spy-lady's daughter. Kristen was content to feast her eyes on the bar-keeper's son.

After a few minutes more of general conversation, Jacob excused himself to continue his chores, straightening chairs, wiping off tables, and, as more patrons began to straggle in, he even stepped behind the bar, pulling drafts of ale into clean mugs. Another man came into the tap from another back room and took charge behind the bar. It was difficult to determine his age, but Kristen would have pegged it as somewhere in his forties. Hard to tell though, with the unkempt grey hair and lined face. People didn't seem to age well, back in the day.

Her eye wandered back to Jacob, who was talking animatedly with two men who sat at a table across the room. So cute. So capable and personable. So… colonial.

Arrgghh. It was more than she could conceive that she was here making sheep's eyes at some boy whose great-great-great-great-many-times-great grandson went to school with her brother. The fact that Jacob Tyson, who stood not ten feet away from her, was in actuality long dead and buried was both creepy and mind-blowing.

The clatter of Brad's cup on the table brought her out of her reverie.

Kristen cleared her throat. "Man, it's kind of odd to see someone our age working in a bar, serving drinks," she observed.

"Yeah, but I'm pretty sure there are no child labor laws to worry about, not to mention there probably isn't even an official legal drinking age."

"I suppose when kids get to be about our age, they had no choice but to go to work somewhere. No more schooling, no hanging out with friends. No place *to* hang out, even if they had time. What do you suppose they do for fun?"

Brad shrugged. "Barn dances? Quilting bees? Gathering together behind a covered bridge somewhere with a jug of something borrowed from their parents' storeroom?"

"Or gather *under* a bridge," Kristen replied with a mischievous grin. "Or, to make a modern reference, under a highway overpass. Or behind an abandoned building. In other words, same stuff that goes on in our time."

"Yeah, the same stuff: the six-packs, someone with a pack of smokes, the car sound systems blasting away… Yep, just the same old stuff. Except it's not exactly old at the moment, now, is it? It's unheard of at this point. Futuristic, even. Waaaay off in the future."

Both were silent for a moment, thinking about their 'real' lives. What was going on in their timeline? Did anyone know they were gone? If they were here, in the past, did anyone in the future even remember them or know they existed? Or had their 'transition' to the past totally erased them from their 'normal' timeline?

More importantly, how would they ever get back there? If they even could, that is. Kristen decided there was no point in worrying about *if*; she was going to concentrate on the *how* and the *when*.

They *would* get back, she decided. She would not accept any other outcome; would not even consider it.

A door closed somewhere toward the back of the tavern, and a moment later Major Clark escorted Rebecca back into the taproom. Brad and Kristen looked at each other; Rebecca looked relieved. She smiled at them, the sort of smile that indicated a burden lifted.

"I thank you, Miss Darrow, for stopping by. Our chat has been most useful," Major Clark said by way of dismissal. "Mr. Tyson will see that you get food and drink as required, and you're free to go."

"So you'll take care of it?" Brad asked. "You'll take the, er, information to General Washington and see that, um, proper precautions are taken."

Timekeepers: A Revolutionary Tale

The major glowered at Brad, drawing himself up to full height and eying the seated teenager. "You, young man, are not involved in this conversation. However, since you accompanied Miss Darrow this far, I will assure you that the General will be apprised of the situation immediately, and we will act with all due propriety to ensure we are prepared for any occurrence." He bowed at the waist slightly. "Your servant, ladies, sir," and then he left them.

Rebecca smiled again. "May I join you? Now that my task has been completed, I find that I'm ravenous."

Brad held a chair for her, and Mr. Tyson himself brought them some apples and something else, which looked like either fat pancakes, or flattened biscuits. Kristen looked at the plate suspiciously, and was about to ask what they were when Brad gestured and asked, "Are those… journey cakes?"

Mr. Tyson nodded. "Of course. Don't you know journey cake when you see it? Or maybe you call it johnnycake?"

"No, we call it, er, journey cake. But I'm just used to it looking a little more…"

"Edible?" Kristen suggested.

"—buttery," Brad finished, darting one of his WBs at his sister. "A little butter makes them a little more, uh, yellow."

"Well, I'd add more butter if I had it," the tavern owner replied, moving on, "but these days I can't make enough butter to have some for every little thing."

"And I'm sure these are great just as they are," Brad said, rather lamely.

Jacob came to refill their mugs, and Rebecca asked if there was any cider. When he said there was, Brad and Kristen quickly indicated they'd like cider, as well. With a shake of his head, Jacob took away their mugs of flip and came back shortly with three mugs of cider before resuming his chores.

Kristen didn't even think to wonder if they were fresh mugs or if the flip had merely been poured out of their previous mugs and the cider poured in; she was very thirsty, and at least cider was something she was familiar with.

Something she could actually drink. Other than the fact that it was room temperature rather than chilled the cider was as refreshing as frozen yogurt on a hot day at the beach.

After a while the three young people rose and thanked Mr. Tyson for his hospitality.

"Oh, don't thank me. I'm glad to do what I can for the cause, and I thank you, young lady, for your efforts. Now, I've been instructed to have you leave by a certain route, and my son Jacob will accompany you."

"Oh, that's not necessary—" Brad began.

"Shhh," Kristen said. "Let the man speak."

"Yes, well," Mr. Tyson continued, "Jacob will show you the best route back to Philadelphia. To avoid the British patrols, don't ya know?"

"Oh, but I have a pass," Rebecca said. "In fact, I'm supposed to be going to Flourtown." She drew out the empty flour sacks she'd put in her satchel.

"Don't worry. The way back will take you past Frankford and some other mills, and you can get your flour there. Them redcoats will never know the difference. And if they ask what took you so long, tell 'em there was flooding on the Frankford Road. Which is true enough this time o' year, eh? Especially after last week's rain."

He gave them some more journey cakes to take with them—this century's version of Go-Gurt or a power bar, Kristen thought. However, before the group set out for the next leg of their whacked-out day, Kristen knew one thing could not be avoided any longer: she had to use the outhouse.

She had Brad make a discreet inquiry of Mr. Tyson, and was soon heading out the back door of the tavern, scowling at her brother, who was obviously enjoying her dread. However, there was nothing to be done except deal with the situation, so she acted as if this was nothing new to her, and went out to do her business.

She had known it would be smelly (or "malodorous," as her mother would have said), but she was pleasantly surprised that it wasn't much worse. She didn't know *why* it wasn't as bad as she had feared, and she really didn't care. The physical discomfort and the darkness in the 'house' were bad enough, and even if it had smelled like a Yankee Candle store, it would still have been an unpleasant experience.

She was glad to rejoin the others, and gladder still about the small bottle of hand sanitizer she had tucked in her backpack before the sleepover last weekend.

The four teens exited the front of the tavern. The ringing anvil of the next-door blacksmith provided accompaniment to their footfalls, but did not totally cover the sound of voices from the vicinity of the stables. Glancing over, Kristen saw Major Clark in conversation with two fellow officers who had apparently just arrived and dismounted... one of whom seemed awfully familiar.

Brad had obviously seen them too.

"Is that....," he began. "Could that really be...?"

"Who?" Jacob asked, turning to see what had captured Brad's attention.

"Washington. It's George Washington. He's a general, and commander of the Continental Army, not to mention being the very first presi-- er, I mean, well— It's General Washington!"

"Yes, we can see that," Kristen replied, tugging on her brother's sleeve. "Now come on, let's not make a scene."

"Not make a scene? I have no intention of making a scene. But dude! I'm a stone's throw away from George Washington. Father of our country! I'd give my right arm to meet and talk to him."

"Well, I'll 'give your right arm,' too—give it a yank right out of the socket if you don't calm down and get moving." She took a mock-serious tone. "Brad, step away from the president."

Reluctantly, Brad turned away, shaking his head at the missed opportunity. Meeting the first President of the United

States? Yeah, that's an opportunity that would never happen again.

The young people retraced their steps down the road the way they had come for a short distance, and then Jacob indicated a path leading into the forest.

"This should bypass most of the long route you took earlier," he said, "and will get us to where the mills are."

"I thank you," Rebecca answered. "I know this area a little, but certainly not as well as you do."

"My pleasure, Miss Darrow. Any time we can pull the wool over the eyes of the lobsterbacks, I'm all for it, and glad to help in any way I can."

"Are they around here much? The lobsterbacks?" Brad asked.

Jacob, who had been in the lead on the narrow path, turned to answer. "For the past six months or so, they've been everywhere. First, General Howe's troops were swarming all about this area, but they were called to action for the battle of Brandywine. Then came the skirmish at Germantown, and they were everywhere again, and they've never left since. Now, with the British occupying Philadelphia, we see a lot of their officers travelling through the area, riding to and from the city to meet with Howe, or what-have-you. Most of which you probably already know, of course."

"Isn't it likely that they have even more scouts out now, since they're planning to, er, take action?" For some reason, Kristen was hesitant to use the word 'attack.' Saying it sounded brutal, and, crazily, might make it come true. Which, of course, she already knew to *be* true. It would happen, and soon. At least, it had better, if history were to play out the way it was supposed to.

Boy, this is weird, she thought. *How often do people— civilians, not soldiers or despots or war-mongers—how often do people* want *to have a battle? A battle in which there will be injuries and deaths. People will die, real people, maybe people I've seen so far today, maybe even William Darrow or*

Timekeepers: A Revolutionary Tale

Major Clark, and yet, this battle has *to happen. And it has to happen just as Brad and I have always heard about it since we were in pre-school.*

Well, we've done our part. If Brad and I are here for a reason, I guess we accomplished it. We escorted Little Miss Revolution to deliver her spy message, so everything should be on track to take place just the way the history books tell me it did.

I hope.

Kristen was darn tired of walking. Again, couldn't the Tysons have had a wagon? Would it kill these people to own a horse or two? She had no idea how far they'd walked, or what time it might be; from the position of the sun, she guessed it had to be after noon. *Dang, listen to me; now I sound like Columbus, or Daniel Boone, or Saca-freakin'-jawea.*

But, if it *was* after twelve, she had a big problem.

Kristen had almost forgotten that she'd asked a question—about the likelihood of the British having a lot of scouts in the area—until Jacob answered it.

"Yes, I reckon they do have a lot of scouts out now, else how would they know where the troops are in order to plan an attack? But one thing we don't want, is for them to get too good a bead on that. Knowing where we are is one thing, and that's water under the bridge now, but knowing how many troops we have—well, that's another kettle of fish, and what we need to avoid if we can."

"Why?" she asked. "They're already going to make a 'surprise' attack, so what difference can it make if they knew many men we have?"

"Well, now, think about it. If you're going to attack me and you know I have five hundred men, how many would you use to attack?"

Brad shrugged. "I don't know, seven hundred and fifty?"

"But if you think I have a thousand men, how many would you bring?"

"If I know you have a thousand, I guess I'd have to bring—" Brad's eyes widened. "—more," he said. "The smaller number the Brits think we have, the fewer men they'll use to attack. But if we actually have more…."

"We have a better chance of matching them man-for-man," Rebecca finished. She gave Jacob a smile. "Very good thinking."

"Don't credit me with it," he said hastily, blushing slightly. "It's the officers who done all the thinkin'. Besides, from what I could gather, General Washington had more or less figured that Howe would attack—you know, trying to 'surprise' us. His scouts and other local patriots have been seeing signs of it for weeks past, so he was pretty sure the attack would come; one last battle before winter sets in, as we've heard that General Howe is desperate for a decisive victory before the snow flies. Now, thanks to Miss Darrow here, General Washington has got some solid information as to when and where it will be."

Now it was Rebecca's turn to blush, causing Kristen to roll her eyes. "It was my mother who learned the details," the colonial girl said, "and at great risk to herself, I might add. I'm just the messenger."

"Okay," Kris said, since it looked like Jacob was about to say something nauseatingly polite and complimentary. "Now that little Susie Spy-Girl has done her James Bond thing, and delivered the secret message, can we just concentrate on where we're going, please? Brad and I have places to be."

Everyone stopped and looked at her.

"We do?" Brad asked.

"Susie Spy-Girl?" Rebecca repeated.

"What is 'okay'?" Jacob inquired.

Kristen rolled her eyes and gave a frustrated sigh. "Ugh! Never mind," she said, starting briskly forward. "Let's just go."

Timekeepers: A Revolutionary Tale

Jacob turned to Brad as they followed behind. "Who is this James Bond?" he asked. "Does he lead one of General Washington's regiments? I don't believe I've met him."

To Kristen, it seemed as if they'd already walked as much that afternoon as they had that morning. Of course, at this point, she was just grumpy in general. Now she was doubly glad she'd worn her sturdy Pumas; this wooded trail was even less hospitable than the dirt tracks they called roads in this backwoods century. Her borrowed dress, too, was showing signs of wear and tear, getting caught on low branches or thorns along the path. The drama teacher was not going to be happy about that.

Not to mention, Kristen had only taken a few bites of that journey cake back at the tavern. It hadn't been too bad—tasted sort of like a pancake—but to her it was inedible without butter or syrup. Plus, it had been served cold... well, actually, at room temperature, not straight off the griddle like she was used to. Between the heavy, bulky clothing, the clunky shoes, the so-so food, the necessity of walking everywhere... it was almost as if these colonials went out of their way to make their lives as uncomfortable as possible.

Kristen knew that Rebecca had some journey cakes in her bag, wrapped up for her by Mr. Tyson at the tavern. *Oh well*, Kristen thought, *I guess that's why they're called journey cakes; you take them "to go" for your journey. I've heard of johnnycakes---seen 'em sold at the county fair a few years ago—I bet they're the same thing. I remember thinking of that nursery rhyme: johnnycake, johnnycake, baker's man.... Wait, that's not right; it's "Pat-a-cake, pat-a-cake." Oh man, I really need to get back to the real world and quit thinking about nursery rhymes and second-rate cardboard breakfast food.*

"Hey, Brad," she asked, "you got one of those apples Mr. Tyson gave us? I could use a bite."

Her brother fished one out of his backpack. "I figure we're going to have to do something soon," he said. "I don't think we can go all the way to Philly with Rebecca."

"Why not? We've already been all over Hell's Half-Acre with her. I feel like we've walked over the whole blasted county."

"Yeah, but remember whose headquarters are in Philly. And who doesn't have one of those precious official passes."

Kristen nodded, "Good point," and took a bite of the Cortland apple. "But what are we supposed to do? I don't know about you, but I'm pretty sure I can't find my way back to the park—or where the park's going to be in the way-too-distant future—to the re-enactment scene where we started."

"I know, me either," he said glumly. "With no recognizable landmarks, we'd have a tough time finding the battle site, or where the fog was." He gave a short laugh. "How's that for irony: if we wait a day or two, we'll find out first-hand exactly where the battle site is. In fact, we'd have front-row seats. But, as it is, until that time, we have no clue. We'll never find it on our own. I'm just hoping something will come to me."

"Yeah, and the crazy thing is—*another* crazy thing, I should say, to add to all the others we've had the joy of experiencing so far today—is that we don't even know how important it is. Or if it's important at all. Just because we were at that park when we jumped time zones, doesn't mean we have to be there in order to get back. We're just sort of assuming that."

Brad gave a snort. "Because we have nothing else to go on. It's our one remote, flimsy thread of hope."

"Well, we have another problem, too. You got any idea what time it is? And so help me, if you look up at the position of the sun and try to tell time like Daniel Boone, I'll smack you."

That caused Brad to smile. "No, I didn't wear my watch since it's not authentic to the period, but—hey, wait a minute.

Duh!" He reached back into his backpack. "We do have a way of telling the exact time." He pulled out his cell phone, checking to be sure that Jacob and Rebecca weren't looking their way.

"Wait, I thought you said we couldn't use our phones."

"We can't. Not as phones or GPS tools; no satellites or cell towers, remember? But the phone function doesn't need any type of wireless connection, so that should work even in these, er, primitive surroundings."

"Right, we should be good as long as the batteries have a charge. Good thinking, techno-geek." She watched him thumb his phone. "And now I'm afraid to ask what time it is."

"Why?"

"'Cuz the O'Neills asked me to babysit tonight, and I told mom I'd let her know by noon whether I was going to do it."

"And you can't call mom."

Kristen didn't even take the opportunity to make a smart remark to Captain Obvious. "When she doesn't hear from me, she'll eventually try to call me."

"And when she can't reach you on your phone...."

"She'll freak. And probably send dad over to the park to find me. And when he *can't* find me—or you, either, because nobody's seen us...."

"*He'll* freak."

"Bingo." Kristen watched Brad drop his phone back into one of the pockets of his backpack. "So what do we do?"

He shrugged. "Honestly, I don't know. What *can* we do? It's not like we did this on purpose, or even know how it happened. And you're right, it's after twelve already."

"Great. So now we're screwed in *two* centuries. Not only is mom freaking two hundred and thirty years in the future, probably within a few miles of where we stand, but on top of all that, we're now walking straight into enemy territory. Yup, that's just teriffic: screwed in two centuries."

She and Brad continued to trudge along behind the two colonials, Rebecca and Jacob. In fact, Kristen felt like she'd been 'trudging' all day. It had been about eight o'clock when she and her brother had arrived at the park for the re-enactment and encountered the mystery fog. And they'd pretty much been walking ever since. In fact, other than the brief respite at the tavern, she hadn't sat down since she'd gotten out of the Corolla that morning.

Man, this should count as a gym credit, as well as community service, she thought. *I've been walking for about four freakin' hours. And the day ain't over yet.*

But, Brad was right, and not, she admitted to herself, for the first time today. She couldn't worry about what was going on, or supposed to be going on, in the twenty-first century. It was pointless, since there was nothing they could do about it. All she and Brad could do was to deal with the here and now. *Ha!* she thought. *The now is supposed to be then, as in 'back then.' Ancient history. But it's not then, it's now. And the here… all she had was a general idea of where 'here' was. Man, this is one whacked-out deal. I still wouldn't be surprised to turn a corner and run straight into real time, with motorcycles and really good pedicures and fast-food restaurants that serve chicken wings. It's just that crazy.*

Suddenly, she saw Jacob stop and raise a hand for silence. The Everhearts stepped softly to catch up to where he stood.

"What do you hear?" Brad asked quietly.

"I thought I heard voices. That way," he pointed off into the trees to the left.

"Is there a road there, or a trail?"

Jacob shook his head, his wavy hair dancing slightly. "Whoever it is, is on foot. You three stay here; let me look."

Kristen put her hand out. "No, don't," she said, also whispering. "You have no idea who's out there."

Jacob gave her a quizzical look. "I know. That's why I'm going to reconnoiter—to see who's out there."

She knew her objection had been silly and that she should feel embarrassed—especially since it caused Jacob to look at her like she was nuts—but suddenly all she really felt was tension. "All I meant was that it could be dangerous," she mumbled.

He smiled, and touched her shoulder lightly. "Don't worry. I know these woods like they were my own house, and I've been hunting since I was five years of age. I know how to move quietly through the trees."

He looked at them all then. "You three stay here. I'll be back in just a few minutes."

With that, Jacob stepped away.

Kristen remembered reading in a book once that a character had 'melted into the shadows.' She'd liked that imagery, and thought it evoked an accurate portrayal of someone being swallowed by darkened shapes.

Now, as she watched Jacob, the most accurate description she could have given would be to say that he melted into the woodland around them, even in daylight. One minute he was there, visible amid the trees, and the next he had disappeared, almost as if by magic.

Brad directed the two girls next to a large tree trunk and set his pack down. "Sit if you'd like," he said quietly.

Kristen sat, if only to get off her feet for a few minutes. Rebecca, apparently made of sterner stuff, continued to stand, glancing occasionally in the direction Jacob had taken.

"I'm sure you'll be glad to get back home," Brad said, as a way to keep her thoughts occupied, in addition to simply helping to pass the time.

"Yes, I suppose," the girl replied, grateful for the distraction. "I must confess I'd rather be doing household chores and helping my mother in the kitchen than skulking around in the forest."

"How long have the British been using your home for meetings?"

"A few months. At first General Howe's man insisted we leave our house altogether, but my mother was able to make a bargain with him. My parents could stay in the house, but the general would use it as a meeting place, or to house extra officers. Either way, my mother has to cook for them." She smiled without humor. "British military officers certainly like their comforts. They hunt and bring in the freshest meats, and enjoy soirees and social events with the Loyalists—just as if they were in London, I'm sure. On top of that, they also raid the pantries and storerooms and wine cellars of some of the fine houses in Philadelphia owned by patriots, which their owners had to abandon when the redcoats took over the city."

Brad gave a hrmph. "While their lower-ranking soldiers eat whatever scraps they can forage, no doubt. And your friends who've been driven out of their homes—do they criticize your mother for serving the British?"

"I don't think so. My family has made sacrifices too. Alice and Liam, my younger sister and brother, were sent to live with relatives in Trenton when the British took Philadelphia. And you've met William; he decided to join the American army. So I think everyone understands the sacrifices my parents have made."

"Do you live in the house too, with your parents?"

"No, I'm staying with friends nearby, although I spend most days helping my mother with her duties. But she doesn't want me anywhere near the British officers once evening comes."

I bet, Brad thought. Many officers in the British army were noblemen: Major Lord This, or Captain Lord That. And many thought that others—those 'below' them—were fair game for whatever whim they wanted to indulge. After all, he'd seen *The Tudors*. Was he generalizing? Maybe. But Brad's mother wouldn't want Kristen walking around Willow Grove Naval Air Base after dark, either, so he could understand Mrs. Darrow's thinking in regard to Rebecca.

Speaking of Kristen, Brad looked over to see her rooting through her backpack. Luckily, Rebecca had her back to his sister, as Kris began to systematically take things out of said pack: paperback book, cellphone, flashlight, something he supposed was some sort of makeup, and the PSP game system.

Finally she must have found what she was looking for, as she then tossed everything else back in the bag. That's right: tossed. Leave it to his sister to take no heed of organization or care of her belongings.

"Hey," Kris said, getting to her feet. "Even though that journey cake was, er, just yummy, anybody want a bite of granola bar?"

"Granola bar? What's that?"

Kristen had actually had the presence of mind to unwrap the bar before offering it to Rebecca and him. And, Brad noticed with admiration (and not a little surprise), she'd apparently read the wrapper before stuffing it in her backpack. Thus, she was able to say, "It's like a snack cake. Made out of grain and nuts—among other things. It's good for you. Sort of."

"Right," Brad said, "although it's not as good for you as an apple. Too much sugar."

Rebecca shrugged. "I can have an apple anytime. Right now I want to try some Prussian food. A granola bar."

She took the piece that Kristen had broken off for her, and sniffed at it curiously. Then she took a bite.

"Mmmm," she said, looking a bit surprised, "that's quite tasty. And sweeter than I thought it would be."

Brad and Kristen looked at each other, and both said "Too much sugar," he with an 'I-told-you-so' tone, and she with a 'yeah-yeah-whatever' tone.

At that moment there was a slight rustling of dry leaves nearby, and suddenly Jacob was standing next to them.

"Wow, how'd you do that?" Kristen asked. "We didn't hear a blasted thing, and suddenly—boom, you're here. Man, you're good!"

"I told you, I've been hunting and tracking for years. And besides," he continued, looking at them censoriously, "you've been too busy talking about granola and sugar to notice my approach."

"Oh, you heard that?" Brad asked, as bit sheepishly.

"Only from a mile away."

"I thought we were whispering," Kristen replied… in a whisper.

"You were whispering loudly," came the reply… in a similar tone.

Rebecca cleared her throat, effectively putting an end to this silly conversation. "What did you see out there?" she asked Jacob.

"Just what I expected to see: redcoat scouts. Two of 'em, and pretty clumsy, I might add. Or maybe just overconfident. They were making as much noise tramping through the trees as a wounded deer."

Kristen didn't want to think about Bambi, hurt in the woods. "Could you hear them talking?"

Jacob nodded, his dirty blond locks bobbing deliciously. "I think they know that General Washington is nearby, but they don't seem to be aware of how many men he has in the area, or the fact that there are more on the way."

"Well, that's good news for us," Brad said. "Er, for you."

"No, 'us' is right," Kristen corrected. "We're definitely with them"—tilting her head to indicate Jacob and Rebecca— "so if we're with them, that means that we are a part of 'us.'"

Everyone looked at her blankly. "What?" she asked defensively. "It makes perfect sense."

"If you say so," Jacob replied. He shook his head. "Anyway, we should be on our way. With luck I should be able to get you to the Frankford mill and back to Philadelphia by sunset."

"Sunset," Kristen repeated. "Yippee."

CHAPTER FOUR

Sunset! That meant the setting of the sun, Kristen thought. When it got dark. As in evening, which leads directly to night. We can't be here then; not at night, and certainly not—sure as *hayell* not—overnight.

It was Saturday, for god's sake. She was supposed to be at the re-enactment until about one o'clock, go home for lunch, then she and Abby were scheduled to go to the library and after that maybe get some fro-yo, and she'd be home by six to eat dinner and be at the O'Neill's by seven-thirty to babysit.

It was supposed to be a normal Saturday: hanging out with friends, putting up with geek-boy brother, talking and texting, spending the evening watching cheesy sci-fi movies once little Daniel O'Neill was safely in his baby bed. Just typical stuff for teenaged girls.

Instead, here she was, playing Time Travel Tammy. Wearing an uncomfortable long dress, carrying or wearing her backpack everywhere, walking mile after mile after friggin' daggone mile.

She didn't even want to think about having to spend the night here. Not without a bunch more provisions. It was fall, and Pennsylvania tends to be chilly this time of year—to say the least!—especially at night; temperatures generally bottomed out in the forties, and it wasn't inconceivable that the low could even dip into the thirties. The drama club's colonial-era dress she was wearing was heavy compared to the sweat-shirt and jeans she'd normally have on, but it wasn't so heavy that it would keep Kristen warm if it got much cooler. So far, the exertions of all this walking had done a lot to keep her warm, but once it got dark, she doubted they'd do much walking. And neither she nor Brad had a coat—oops, make that a cloak to stay in period with the vernacular—to wear over their costumes. In fact, other than a tee- or sweat-shirt or something stuffed in her backpack, Kristen didn't have anything to wear to help her keep warm, and she doubted Brad did either. (Even if he *was* a boy scout, this was one eventuality she was pretty sure that even he hadn't thought to prepare for.)

So, staying overnight here in the woods was a no-go. They couldn't do it—she *wouldn't* do it. Come hell or high water, Kristin Everheart was *not* going to sleep in the great outdoors in an ill-fitting borrowed dress in the middle of the eighteenth century.

In the chill air of autumn.

During the Revolutionary War.

Not. Going. To. Happen.

As Brad had mentioned, they couldn't go to Philadelphia with Rebecca, and they sure weren't going to stay in the woods. Maybe they could go back to the tavern with Jacob and spend the night there if necessary. An actual room to sleep in was probably too much to hope for, but even the taproom had a fireplace; throw a few blankets on the floor and she and Brad could probably survive the night well enough. Although even that would require some clever persuasion, as Jacob was obviously no fool. He'd have to be convinced—and his father, too—that the Everhearts weren't dangerous or untrustworthy.

And there was darn little to make him believe that. There was no reason in the world for anyone—Jacob, his father,

Timekeepers: A Revolutionary Tale

Major Clark—to trust Brad and Kristen. Except the fact that they'd accompanied Rebecca in her quest to deliver important information. That was the only thing the siblings had going for them in this timeline—and that was precious little. After all, to everyone else living in 1777, Brad and Kristen Everheart didn't even exist.

Not to mention the fact that they had run into Rebecca Darrow purely by accident. It's not like they had deliberately set out to help her, not like it had been a purposeful act on their part to get involved in her little secret mission. It just happened that Rebecca had been the first person they'd run into after their, er, arrival. It had just… happened.

Nobody else knew that, of course, and it didn't really matter.

As the four teens walked, Kristen dropped back and reached into her backpack for her cell-phone. The sun dappled through the trees as she checked the time: three-twenty. She sincerely hoped something would happen soon. All this walking and the intrigue of helping Rebecca deliver her message was one thing; at least it had kept her occupied, given her something to do, something on which to focus her energy

. But she really, really, *really* wanted to go home. She wouldn't let Brad see it, but she was worried about how that was going to happen. And scared that it wouldn't. What if missing person reports weren't all abductions or accidents? What if some of them were the result of people encountering these…anomalies, these funky time-shifting fogs, and being sucked into another point in time? Amelia Earhart? She could be living like a queen in medieval Italy. Jimmy Hoffa—transported to the Han dynasty in China. Even D.B. Cooper, the guy who jumped out of an airplane with two-hundred-thousand dollars in ransom money, and was never seen again... who knows, maybe he materialized on one of Columbus' ships and became one of the 'discoverers' of America.

Well, okay, maybe not. A little too fanciful of a theory, the kind of geeky sci-fi stuff Brad would believe in. *I'm just getting a little punchy*, she thought.

Kris became aware that the others were talking, and, looking ahead through the trees, she could see yet another dirt road. Catching back up to the others, she heard Jacob point out that Frankford Mill was just up the road to the north, and once Rebecca had gotten her flour, taking the road back the opposite way—south—would lead directly to Philadelphia.

"Yes, I know this road," Rebecca said. "Germantown Road. Once I get my flour from the mill, I know how to get back to the city."

"I'll walk with you--all of you--until you near the city," Jacob said.

"That would be nice," she replied, her cheeks pinking a bit. "But it's not really necessary. I do know the way, and you need to get back to the tavern."

Jacob smiled at her, a crooked grin which showed surprisingly nice teeth. For someone who didn't have access to a Waterpik or baking-soda toothpaste or whitening strips, he sure had a nice smile.

"Well, my job was to see that you, er, that is, the *three* of you, get back to Philadelphia, and that's what I'm going to do."

"Uh yeah, about that… see, we're not going to Philadelphia," Brad broke in. Good thing he did, too, since neither of these two seemed to remember that he and Kristen were even there.

Jacob blinked and turned to look at Brad. "You're what? Not going to Philadelphia? Why not?"

Rebecca too seemed to snap out of her entrancement. "That's right," she said, consciousness and memory seeming to come back to her. "You said you were going to get flour, too. Then you have to go back to-- to…."

"Er, Falls Village," Brad said. To Kristen, he muttered, "That is what I said earlier, isn't it? Falls Village?"

64

"How should I know? I thought we were from Germany."

"Prussia."

"Whatever." Kristen spoke up, addressing Jacob and Rebecca. "Brad's right, we can't go to Philadelphia. We have to stay here in the woods, preferably back where we first ran into you," indicating Rebecca.

"Why would you have to stay in the woods?" Rebecca asked.

"Uhh, I don't know... we were raised by wolves?"

Brad smacked his sister's arm and rolled her eyes. "Of course we weren't raised by wolves," he told the others. "But we do have to go back to where we found you. We're—er, we're meeting someone there. Later."

Jacob looked at them, confused. "Why would you meet someone in the forest?"

"Because..." Brad wracked his brain—and came up empty.

"See?" Kristen hissed at him. "Being raised by wolves is sounding better and better."

Brad shook his head and ignored her, saying to Jacob, "Just because, that's why. We can't tell you anything more because it's all confidential."

"Yeah, very hush-hush," Kristen added.

"So," Jacob said, "you can't go to Philadelphia because you have to go back into the forest to meet someone, in the dark, and it's a big secret."

"Yeah, that's it."

"On the nose."

"Well, this secret mission of yours... meeting someone deep in the woods... sounds like the work of a spy."

Brad laughed. "When you say it like—wait. What?"

"No, no, no," Kristen said. "We are *so* not spies. We're as American as you are. Born and raised here—just miles away, in fact. Not to mention a few centuries. But believe me, we're big fans of George Washington."

"And we really, really, really want him to kick General Howe's ass at White Marsh the day after tomorrow," Brad added. "It's very important that he win that battle and lead the American troops to defeat the British."

Kris nodded. "After all, how else is he gonna become president and get on the dollar bill?"

Whereas a moment ago Jacob was looking at them suspiciously, now he looked just plain confused. "What? Washington is going to become what, and get on where? I have no idea what you're talking about."

Brad gave Kristen another of his WB looks. "Welcome to my world. Look, I know it sounds crazy—and it is, I admit. But the reality is, we do have to go back to where we first met Rebecca. It's the only way we can get home."

"Get home? If you're lost, I'm sure I can—"

"We *are* lost," Kristen said, sighing. "No two ways about that. And, unfortunately for us, even the best hunter and tracker in the world—your world—can't get us home."

Jacob opened his mouth to reply, but Rebecca grabbed his arm. "Shhh! Listen," she said.

They all heard it: twigs breaking, leaves rustling. Someone was not too far off, and not being very quiet about it.

Kristen was shocked to see Jacob pull a knife out from beneath his cloak while with his other hand he put his fingers to his lips. He cocked his head in an attitude of listening, and then slipped silently among the trees.

"We may have to hide," Brad said quietly.

"Hide!" Kristen repeated in a whisper. "Where? How? We're not hobbits; we don't have cloaks that conveniently camouflage us."

"I know, but—" Brad's reply was cut off by Jacob's reappearance. They all looked at him questioningly.

"Not soldiers," he said curtly. "At least not at the moment. They may be deserters."

"Deserters! What should we do?" Rebecca asked, clearly looking to Jacob for guidance.

Timekeepers: A Revolutionary Tale

"There are some evergreen trees over yonder. Judging from the direction those men were taking, they may pass nearby, and the trees I mentioned offer the best cover."

It was late autumn, and most leaves had fallen from the trees, which to this point made for some pretty noisy walking as dry leaves weren't exactly quiet when rustled underfoot. However, Kristen didn't recall seeing any Christmas trees in this forest. That's what she thought of when Jacob said 'evergreens,' and a nice eight-foot tree certainly would be wide enough for them to hide behind. Add a little tinsel and some ornaments—not to mention a star on top—and yeah, they'd be practically invisible.

They crept as quietly as possible as they followed Jacob, carefully picking their feet up rather than shuffling leaves in their wake. Sure enough, there were a couple of evergreen trees up ahead, and Kristen mentally kicked herself for forgetting where she was.

These were Eastern hemlocks, which species she had known since the third grade was the state tree of Pennsylvania. Duh!

The conifers were pretty young, probably no more than twenty feet tall. Even with the fully-needled branches, which started about three or four feet off the ground, the trees couldn't completely hide the four teenagers from sight of the passersby, but they would do well enough.

Kristen forced herself next to one tree with Jacob at her side. He maneuvered her as near to the trunk as the thick limbs would allow, and crowded close to her, trying to make them both seem part of the tree. A quick glance told her that Brad and Rebecca were similarly situated next to the other tree.

Any other time, she'd probably enjoy this: a good-looking guy pressing himself against her, smelling as he did of woodsmoke and the outdoors. Kristen's eyes were about level with his chin, and she could see the stubble on his cheek, as well as a small cut along his jawline, probably from the last time he'd shaved. He was close enough that she could feel his chest move as he breathed, and if she'd had room to put her hand up, she could probably feel his heart thumping beneath the brown woolen cloak.

She found herself taking shallow breaths, not because she was literally 'breathless,' or that Jacob's proximity 'took her breath away,' but because she was almost afraid that if she breathed normally, with full, deep breaths, she would practically push him away. He was *that* closely pressed against her.

One of Jacob's hands was braced against the trunk of the tree, and the other rested lightly on the hilt of the knife in its sheath. Under other circumstances, Kristen would say he had her pinned against the tree, and it would be true, but there was nothing romantic about it. Or menacing, for that matter. 'Shielding' would be the more accurate term. His dark brown coat and breeches were as much camouflaging as she could hope for as she stood with her back against the scratchy bark.

Brad and Rebecca were in a similar case. He had his arm on the Quaker girl's shoulder, pressing her as close to the tree trunk as possible. And yet he wasn't standing as near to her as Jacob stood to Kristen. The thought flew fleetingly through Kris' mind that Brad, even while stuck in a time-warp, hiding from renegade deserters in the darkening forest, was ever the gentleman, being careful not to crowd Rebecca.

Jacob apparently had no such qualms with her. Not that he was being disrespectful… apparently it didn't occur to him that it could be construed that way. *That'll teach me*, she thought, *to try to apply twenty-first century sensibilities to an eighteenth century situation.*

No, Jacob was all about the mission, which was protecting those who had been put in his charge: in this case, the "womenfolk." Kris smiled to herself at that thought. Little did Jacob Tyson know that she'd taken two years of karate at the "Y" when she was younger, and that she'd successfully beat the snot out of Tony Krocker when he'd deliberately tripped her friend on the playground in the third grade.

Well, never mind. If Jacob's sense of honor dictated that he press her against a tree trunk with his body, so that their very breaths mingled warmly and haltingly between them… who was she to argue the point?

The sound of voices and rustling leaves grew steadily closer, until it almost sounded as if the rogues were on the other side of the tree.

"I ain't doin' it, Bob," said one angrily. "It ain't right."

"You want right, or do you want money?" came the reply from 'Bob.' "All's we have to do is snoop around the camp some. Don't ye want t' get paid? That's why we hoofed it out of there to begin with—the army ain't paid us."

"So why're we still crawling around the countryside? I say we just go home to our families."

To Kristen's horror, the strangers seemed to have stopped to argue. Her gaze flew to Jacob; his thickly-lashed eyes were glued past her, looking instead through the branches to some point beyond the tree. His face was a study in concentration.

"Go home to our families! With what?" asked Bob. "We ain't got no money, our families ain't got no money, since we weren't there to work the harvest. Nobody's got no money. Except them Brits. When that redcoat officer caught us stealing them eggs, he could've kilt us, or clapped us in irons. But he wants to pay us, Walt. Pay us good money, just for a little snoopin'."

"Yeah, and never mind what happens if we gets caught. First desertin' and then spyin'. That'll work out great for us, Bob. Listen, I saw a clearing over there; I'm going to sit down and maybe get off my feet for a bit. These dogs are barkin'."

"Wait, you don't want to be lolly-gaggin' in these woods—'specially not now when it's comin' dark. Who knows what-all lives in the forest. By which I'm talking about wild animals."

"If something's out there, it ain't gonna come near no fire. Now look for some kindlin'.."

There was some leaf rustling as the two men moved away from the hemlock trees. Kristen felt a rush of air as Jacob let out a deeply-held breath. He peered cautiously around the tree, eyes darting this way and that as he ensured the men were indeed gone.

As Jacob stepped away, Brad and Rebecca trod quietly over to where he and Kristen stood.

"Well, that was close," Brad whispered.

"Yeah, the last thing we need is to be caught by some cowardly deserters," Kristen agreed. "These woods *are* dangerous."

"I doubt they would have physically harmed us," Jacob put in.

"How do you know? I'm sure they were armed, weren't they?"

"One of them did have a musket."

"See?"

"Which posed no threat to any of us."

"How can you know that?" Brad asked curiously.

Jacob shook his head. "No ammunition. Do you really think they would bother stealing eggs from some farm if they had the means to take down a deer or even a rabbit?"

"Good point."

"They probably still have knives," Kristen said, eying Jacob meaningfully. "Apparently everyone around here carries a knife."

"You're right," he replied. "Most men who walk in the woods carry knives. It's a reasonable thing to do. But I don't think those men pose a big threat—not physically, anyway. Not to us."

"What do you mean?"

"Didn't you hear them?" Rebecca put in. "They were talking about spying. On General Washington."

"Yeah, but old buddy Walt over there wasn't on board with the plan. He didn't want to do it," replied Kristen.

"Maybe not," said Jacob. "But think about it. Which of those two do you think would win out in the end?"

"Bob *was* pretty persuasive," Brad said thoughtfully. "For them the choice is between going home empty-handed to face a cold, hungry winter, or taking a risk in helping spy for the British and getting paid a tidy sum for a couple days' work."

"So you think eventually Bob would win out."

Jacob tipped his head. "I don't think he would do it alone, without his friend, but of the two, he has a better chance of convincing the other one. He had more persuasive arguments on his side."

"Okay," Kristen said, "now we know that good ol' Bob gets to be captain of the debate team. So what does that mean for us?"

Jacob and Brad looked at each other as if seeking affirmation that the other would agree with him. They were each about to speak when—

"We have to stop them."

The boys looked at Rebecca in surprise.

Kristen laughed. "She totally stole your thunder. You go, girl!" Kris stuck out her closed hand for a fist bump, then dropped it when Rebecca just looked at her as if she were crazy. Kristen cleared her throat. "Yeah, okay. Anyway. So, what do we do to stop them?"

CHAPTER FIVE

"Keeping these deserters from spying on General Washington may not be as easy as we think," Rebecca said. "They may be desperate."

"I doubt that. They seemed more hungry than dangerous," Brad replied. "Maybe we can befriend them and offer whatever food we have left. The journey cakes, for example."

"And do what, wait for them to fall asleep while they're chewing the blasted things?" Kristen asked.

"No," Jacob replied, his hand on his knife, "once one or two of us have their attention with the food, the rest of us get the upper hand and tie them up."

"And do what with them once we've gotten them tied up?" wondered Kristen. "Assuming that works, for starters, because really, does anyone really think they'd fall for that? But seriously, what would we do then, once we've gotten them tied up—take them back to Washington? What would his officers do to those guys, if they really are deserters?"

Jacob shrugged. "They would most likely be flogged."

"Flogged," Brad repeated.

"Yes. I believe deserters can get up to one hundred lashes."

Timekeepers: A Revolutionary Tale

"Lashes," Kristen said, "as in, with a whip?"

Brad said, "If that's what they'd get for deserting, what about for the spying? I mean, I know they haven't actually spied yet, and maybe they won't anyway, but I can only imagine what the Army officers would do just knowing these guys had thought about it."

"And is that what we want?" Kristen continued. "Bob and Walt may be cowards, but they're also desperate—not just for themselves, but for their families. And besides, if their hitches working for the army are up and they haven't been paid and they're worried about their families, how can anyone blame them? Well, okay, so we can blame them for considering spying—that's just wrong. And for running out on their army buddies in the middle of the night or whatever, 'cuz that's wrong too, but still, I don't want to be responsible for anyone being whipped. Or lashed, or flogged, whatever it's called."

"So do you have a better idea as to how to keep them from informing the British of the strength of the American forces?"

Kris bit her lip speculatively. "Well, as a matter of fact… I think I do. Especially since we don't have to actually interfere with them; all we really need to do is delay or distract them. Brad, this will be a job for you and me, requiring our special skills."

"Um, excuse me, our 'special skills'? Do you want to elaborate on what, exactly, those are?"

"You'll see. You'll just have to trust me."

He laughed. "Trust you! Last time I trusted you, I was eight years old, and you told me my GI Joe action figure would be able to swim back to the top if you flushed him down the toilet."

"Well, he was supposed to be a Navy SEAL GI Joe; he should have known how to swim against the current. And I was, what, six? And you believed me?"

Her brother just shook his head. "What's this plan of yours?

"Whatever you're thinking," Jacob put in, "I can't let you do it. Not the two of you, alone."

"Ha! First of all, like you can stop us. Second of all, you have to stand down on this one. It has to be us, Brad and me. You and Rebecca can't be involved."

The two colonials looked at each other. "Why not?" Rebecca asked. "We *are* involved, and have been all along. What are you trying to hide from us?"

"Let's just say we're trying to protect you."

Before Rebecca could ask "Protect us from what?" which is exactly what she was about to do, Kristen looked at Brad, "I hope you have the proper school spirit."

He looked at his sister questioningly, and she whispered a few words to him. His face cleared in understanding.

"Not bad," he said approvingly. "I think that has a shot at working. At least, better than your swimming GI Joe idea."

To Jacob and Rebecca, he said, "Kristen is right. This plan can work, but the two of you have to stay here. No matter what you hear, don't move until Kris and I come back."

Jacob looked really stressed out and unhappy about this turn of events, which Kristen hated, but there was no way he could help them. This plan had to be carried out by Brad and her. She also wasn't keen on leaving Jacob alone with Revolutionary Rita, but there was no other choice. Besides, it's not like she was involved with Jacob—or ever could be. With any luck, she and Brad would be gone soon *(please, God, please let us be gone soon!)*, and she'd never see him again. His bones would be crumbling in whatever was left of a pine box by the time even her grandparents were born.

Brad and Jacob conferred briefly on where the deserters likely went, and then Jacob joined Rebecca in sitting at the base of one of the hemlock trees. The two Everhearts, meanwhile, set off quietly into the woods.

Once they were safely out of earshot, Brad stopped. "Okay, this is far enough. Let's test it out first, and then we'll strategize."

They reached into their bags and brought out their cell phones. After checking a few settings, they were satisfied and ready.

"Listen," Brad whispered, "I think I hear Bob and Walt talking. There they are."

Sure enough, about fifty or sixty yards away, Kristen saw the two men in a small area where there were no large trees. Through the darkening shadows she could see they were gathering kindling and putting it into a pile.

"I can't believe they're stupid enough to light a fire."

"Why? The trees are so thick, the flames won't be visible unless you get right on top of them."

"Yeah, but the smoke will be visible above the trees from miles away, even in a night sky. Not to mention the smell of the smoke."

"True. Not the brightest move for a couple of guys who are running away from one army, and trying to be stealthy spies for the other one."

"Okay, so here's the plan," Brad said. "I'm going to circle around to the ten o'clock position. You'll be at eight o'clock—"

"You just can't let that GI Joe military thing go, can you?"

"Come on, be serious. You know what I'm talking about or not?"

Kristen sighed. "Yes. We're going to get between the Doofus Brothers and the direction of the tavern and where Washington's army is. Then we're going to unleash the secret weapon."

"Right. I'll signal you to let you know I'm in position. With luck, they'll go running back the way they came."

Kristen followed her brother until she was in position, and watched him pick his way toward his location. She found herself holding her breath, her heart pounding. She felt as if she could sprint a mile, or five miles, or all the way back to the tavern—however far that was. That was the adrenaline, of course; Kristen wasn't one to break into a sprint under normal circumstances; not that she couldn't--she'd run track, after all-- it was just that she had to be properly motivated.

She had already donned her backpack the correct way, with a strap over each shoulder. Most people didn't bother to do that, usually just slipping a single strap over one shoulder. Which totally defeated the purpose of a backpack, which was to distribute the weight of the pack even between the shoulders, thus making it easier to carry. Not to mention decreasing the pressure on the carrier. It made perfect sense, Kristen thought.

She had slipped her arms through the straps and secured the latch across her ribs. This would make it easier to run if their plan went south. In fact, even if the plan succeeded, she and Brad may have to do some sprinting through the woods; that would be a lot easier to do without having to lug a backpack in one hand.

Kristen could hear the muted voices of Bob and Walt as they bickered in the small clearing ahead. She dared to peek from behind the thick trunk of the oak tree next to which she was standing, and saw Bob sitting on the ground while Walt fussed with a pile of kindling. He looked around nervously from time to time, as if half-expecting to be confronted at any moment.

She heard a low whistle, and used the same whistle in return. It was a "birdcall" their father had used on family camping trips when the kids were younger. Dad always thought he was being clever, a real outdoorsman; no birds ever 'replied' to his call, mainly because he had made it up, but to him it sounded like a bird's call, and he was content to add it to the cacophony of nature's sounds, authentic or not.

Timekeepers: A Revolutionary Tale

As soon as Kristen answered Brad's faux-bird call, she thumbed her phone, putting it at its loudest setting, and then accessed the agreed-upon ringtone.

A panther's growl cut into the sounds of the forest. It was echoed a few seconds later by another one, about thirty yards away to Kristen's left.

From behind the tree, she saw the two deserters start and look around. Kristen clicked her phone again and the panther gave another menacing growl.

She heard the sound of movement in the forest, coming toward her from where Brad had been. Kristen too shuffled her feet in the leaf-covered ground, and shaking nearby branches and shrubs, purposely making as much noise as possible from her place behind the big tree. Peeking around the trunk again and into the clearing, she could see that Bob and Walt were scared witless.

Walt dropped the small branches he'd been holding, and looked at Bob. Bob scrambled to his feet and backed up against the nearest tree trunk, scanning the woods wildly.

At that moment another roar from the panther sounded, a little closer this time. Kristen initiated an answering roar of her own. She rustled more leaves and branches.

As soon as she saw Brad move to a tree nearby, she nodded at him and darted to another tree herself, closer to the clearing. She made sure to make as much noise as possible in doing so. This time the panther gave a low growl, rather than a fearsome roar, and the effect was almost more menacing than the louder sound. Behind her she heard Brad shuffling to the cover of yet another tree.

By now Walt and Bob were beyond terrified, their faces plainly pale, even in the late afternoon sunlight filtering through the trees.

"What do we do, Bob? I ain't gonna stay in this forest to be eaten by no wildcat."

"Me neither. I reckon we can go back to town and find someplace to stay the night—someplace with walls, or at least a fence. Then we can light out for Washington's camp again in the morning."

Walt tried to peer into the forest. "You still think that's a good idea? Maybe we should reconsider that plan." He turned to look at his friend, but Bob was already gone, leaving small shrubbery twitching in his wake.

"Bob?" said Walt uncertainly, a tremor in his voice.

Another big cat growl. More shuffling leaves.

Walt turned and hightailed it after his comrade.

Kristen brought out one last roar, and whacked some nearby branches for good measure. Brad ran past her, kicking leaves freely as he made his way to where the two deserters had been. Kristen joined him. Up ahead they could hear sounds of someone crashing through the woods in hasty flight.

"Now that was fun," she said, grinning broadly.

"It was kind of exciting, wasn't it?" her brother agreed. "Good thinking on your part."

"Thanks. It's just a good thing we had our mascot ringtone loaded to our phones."

"Yeah, and it's a good thing we're the Port Barton Panthers. I don't think they would have been quite as intimidated if we were, say, the Drexel High Cardinals."

Kristen's adrenaline was pumping, and she had to take some deep breaths to try to calm herself and slow her racing heartbeat. She was glad to have the opportunity to 'walk it off' and get her breathing back to normal as she and Brad picked their way through the forest back to where Jacob and Rebecca were waiting.

"Well?" Jacob asked, standing when he saw them. "Did your plan work?"

"Oh yeah," replied Brad. "They're gone, at least until tomorrow."

"Tomorrow it won't matter. By then I'll have warned the officers, and General Washington's scouts will be sent out to look for a couple of deserters."

Timekeepers: A Revolutionary Tale

"So what was your plan, anyway?" Rebecca asked curiously. "What did you do?"

"Depends. What did you hear?"

The girl shrugged. "We just heard some sort of commotion in the forest."

"A commotion?" Kristen asked.

"Yes. Some noise—I'm not sure what it was, maybe some sort of animal. And then the sound of someone—or something—moving through the trees."

"Running, more like," Jacob put in.

"Well, there was no animal," Brad assured them. "We just made them think there was. No animal and no danger. Those men are gone, baby, gone."

Kristen took a deep breath. "So, what do we do now?"

Rebecca held up her empty sack. "I still have to get flour."

"Right. We were on our way to—where was it?" Brad looked questioningly at Kristen.

"I don't know. Something to do with… hot dogs? Or wieners?"

"No, frankfurters," Brad said. "That was it--frankfurters."

"Frankford," Jacob cut in. "We were heading to the mill at Frankford."

"Close enough," Kristen said. "Lead on, MacDuff."

When Jacob looked at her questioningly, she said, "That was a line by a very famous writer, William Shakespeare. You might have heard of him, he lived in England about—let me think—oh, a hundred and fifty, sixty years ago."

Brad rolled his eyes. "While I'm impressed with the attempt, you should know that Shakespeare never wrote 'Lead on, MacDuff.' It's a misquote. A very common one, possibly, but a misquote just the same."

"Okay, then how about… lead on, Davy Crockett."

"Wrong century. Not born yet."

"Ummm, Lewis and Clark?"

"About twenty five years early."

"Daniel Boone."

"That'll work."

"Daniel Boone," Jacob said. "I've heard of him. He's been involved in some of the skirmishes with the Indians down in Kentucky. Do you know him?"

Brad just laughed and shook his head.

The four teens continued walking through the forest. Kristen found herself walking with Jacob, while Brad and Rebecca fell in behind.

"So you're strangers to these parts," Jacob said.

Kristen realized these were just about the first words Jacob had directed solely to her since she'd met him. "Well, yes and no," she replied. "We've actually been here before—or near here, anyway. But it's not the same now."

"So it was long ago, then, when you were here."

"Yeah, it seems like a lifetime ago. About five lifetimes, actually."

"You and your brother have an odd way of speaking. You say 'yeah' rather than 'yes,' for example."

Kristen smiled. "Yeah, I guess that would seem strange to you."

"And the word 'okay,' which I understand means 'fine' or 'very well.' Maybe I'll start using that, too."

"No, don't," Kristen said. "It doesn't suit you. I don't think you should change the way you speak. Not because of us."

"Between the way you speak, and the packs that you carry over your shoulders, it would be easy to believe that you come from some very strange place."

"We do. At least, *you* would think it was strange."

"I can honestly say that I've never met anyone quite like you. Er, I mean, the two of you, of course. And I assume you might think the way *we* live is strange."

"Again, yes and no. It's strange in that it's not something we're used to. But that doesn't mean it's strange in a bad way. Just… different." Kristen paused for a moment and then thought it best to change the subject. "So, what do you do when you're not working at the tavern? Or are you always working at the tavern?"

"Well, things have changed since the war began. We used to live normal lives: have lessons, be with our families, have fun from time to time, occasionally we'd take time away to go to dances or social affairs and play games. But now... most of the men have joined the Continental Army, and even a lot of the boys my age."

"How come you haven't?" Kristen asked. Walking through the woods in the darkening autumn afternoon was not something she would have thought to enjoy—at least, the twenty-first-century her wouldn't have enjoyed it; she'd rather be at the mall—but she was enjoying this, both the walk and the company. She wished it could go on, for two major reasons: one, it was just plain enjoyable; after all, what's not to like about a walk through the peaceful woods on such a gorgeous autumn day... especially with a cute, intriguing boy? And two, she was afraid to think about what came next, what would happen when the pleasant walk was over and they reached their destination, as they inevitably would. The longer she could put off thinking about and dealing with that, the better.

Which brought her back to asking Jacob why he hadn't joined the army to fight in the war.

He shook his dark blond curls. "I don't know, really. I should have. My mother says I'm not old enough, yet others my age—my friends, even—have joined. I just think she doesn't want me to leave."

Kristen smiled. "That's only natural. Most mothers don't want their children to do something that could be dangerous. They'd be very proud of them if they did, but still, moms want their sons to stay safe."

"Moms?"

"Mothers."

Jacob nodded, by now apparently getting a little used to the unusual words and phrases of the Everhearts. "Anyway, my father needs my help at the tavern. And Major Clark has me run errands for him from time to time, delivering messages and such like."

"Ah, yes, the spy master."

"He prefers the term Intelligence Officer. And I never carry any secret information; just the usual kinds of messages from one military officer to another."

"Do the British ever come to the tavern?"

"Oh, yes. We're on a main road, and we serve good ale and strong whiskey. And when the king's men come in, we make sure they have plenty of it."

"And you probably also make sure there are ears to listen, in case their lips are loosened to the point at which they say something interesting."

Jacob smiled and shrugged. "If a few lobsterbacks are in their cups and getting talkative, 'tis no fault of ours. We provide the liquor, Miss Everheart. What they do—or say— once they consume it… well, that's their problem."

Kristen smiled. The old "get-'em-drunk-and-loosen-their-tongues" trick. Where better to employ it than a country tavern? She could see Major Clark sitting in a corner, dressed like a poor country yokel, supposedly three sheets to the wind, soaking up whatever an unsuspecting British soldier might say. Or perhaps Jacob's father employs a pretty tavern wench, skilled in asking just the right questions as she serves the next tankard.

Yeah, this Revolutionary War business wasn't nearly as boring in real life as it seemed in the history books. Lots of cool stuff and intrigue was taking place, mostly behind the scenes, and most people would never even know about it.

A few yards behind, her brother and Rebecca were having their own interesting conversation.

"So, do you like living in Philadelphia?" Brad asked.

Timekeepers: A Revolutionary Tale

Rebecca shrugged. "I've lived here all my life. I do love the city; it's so big, and has so much going on. But obviously things were different—better—before the war."

Brad's mind was still stuck on the "so big, so much going on" thing.

Big? If he remembered correctly, Philadelphia had a population of about twenty- or twenty-five thousand during this time period. In his world, that wouldn't even rate as a mid-sized 'burg. But it *was* the most populated city in the colonies, he remembered, and second only to London in the British Empire at the time.

Everything is relative, I guess.

And 'so much going on'? Brad chuckled to himself; Rebecca had no idea. Current residents of Philadelphia sometimes bemoan the fact that 'there's nothing to do' in their city; this, despite the fact that there were four professional sports teams, an orchestra, umpteen museums, a zoo, numerous parks, concerts, festivals… the list went on and on. People in the twenty-first century always seem to overlook what is under their very noses, Brad knew, no matter where they live. They take so many things for granted.

Not to mention, some people are never satisfied, no matter how much they have at their very fingertips.

"What did you like to do before the war?" he asked.

Rebecca tucked a strand of hair that had come loose back behind her ear. "I just liked to walk around the city. From what I understand, it's very unique in the layout."

"The layout?"

"Yes. The grid pattern; no other city in the colonies is configured that way. Also, there is Mr. Franklin's library, the State House, and dozens of shops. I also love the waterfront, and watching the ships come and go; there's always so much going on there."

Once again, Brad was stuck on 'so much going on.' He mentally shook himself, and became aware that Kristen and Jacob had stopped, and as he and Rebecca caught up to them, he realized there was a road up ahead, just outside of the woods.

Jacob indicated one direction, north. "This is the way to Frankford Mill," he said.

"Well, then that's the direction I need to take," said Rebecca. "Then I'll come back this same way and the road will take me to Philadelphia. It's only a few miles south, in the other direction."

Jacob turned to the Everhearts. "You're not going to either the mill or Philadelphia?"

"No, we'd best not," Brad replied. "But we'll wait for you to get back from the mill."

"We will?" Kristen asked in surprise.

He looked at her, eyebrows raised. "You got somewhere else you need to be?"

She gave a snort. "Not at the moment. Not here."

"Are you sure?" Rebecca asked. "I hate the thought of leaving you in the forest to wait. Especially at this time of day."

"We'll be fine," Kristen said. "You two go ahead."

Still skeptical, Jacob and Rebecca set off toward the mill. The Everhearts found a large-boled tree near the road with some scraggly shrubbery growing near the base. Together they provided sufficient cover for the siblings to sit down, yet still be out of sight from the road.

"Man, what I wouldn't give for a couch right about now," Kristen said, stretching her legs out as if she were indeed reclining on a couch. "Add some nachos and salsa and a Dr. Who marathon, and I'd be in heaven."

"For me, you can skip the nachos. Dr. Who is good, though. Nice touch."

"Yeah, but only the David Tennant episodes."

"Ha! Figures you'd like those. Now if only we could find a Tardis and step out of it in our own time zone." Brad checked his cellphone. "Getting late. Probably an hour or so until sunset."

"Not that you could tell that with all these friggin' trees around," Kristen replied. "I can barely tell where the sun is, to determine the direction, or where it's going to set."

"Let's see, Philly is that way, right down the road apiece, or so we've been told. And since where we originally started is a bit northwest of the city… well, I figure we'd want to head in that general direction," he said, pointing.

"Terrific. Our target is somewhere within a twenty-square-mile area, in that general direction," she said. "We think."

"I know," Brad said with a sigh. "We're totally boned. And I bet it's going to get wicked cold tonight."

"La la la…. I'm trying not to think about that," Kris warned.

"Sorry."

After a minute of silence, she said, "I wouldn't mind seeing Philly, though. How often do you get to see your hometown as it was two hundred and forty years ago?" She turned to look speculatively at the road. "It's only a couple miles that way, isn't it?"

"Don't even think about it."

"Why not? I can zip down that way a mile or so, and I should be able to see it from there."

"Doubt it."

"Doubt it? Why?" Kristen asked. "If I walk a mile down the road, it'll only be another mile or so from there. It's not like I'm going to go into the city and do some shopping. I just want to see it."

Brad shook his head. "You're not thinking. *Our* Philadelphia, yes, it's huge, with tall buildings, and you can see it from miles away. But *this* Philadelphia… not so much. It's tiny in comparison. And the tallest building probably isn't more than four stories high."

Kristen sighed. "Good point. I didn't think of that. Although wouldn't it be kind of cool to see some of the buildings we know as historic landmarks, when they're brand new? Like Independence Hall, for one."

"Which of course isn't called Independence Hall in this time period."

"Right, it was the… wait, don't tell me! The Pennsylvania State House building, wasn't it?"

Brad nodded. "Very good. Let's see, what else would we recognize? Christ Church."

"Yup. A couple other churches, too. Old St. Mary's, for one. Old St. Joe's, for another." She laughed. "Which aren't 'old' in this time period, at all."

"Yeah," Brad said thoughtfully, "it would be kind of cool to see the city now. Too bad we don't have a pass to—"

He put up his hand warningly, and then brought his finger to his lips.

Kristen listened. "Footsteps!" she whispered. "They're back already?" She put her hands on the ground beside her, bracing herself to get up.

Brad, seated next to her, put his hand out in front of her.

"No! Listen. The steps are coming from the other direction."

He was right. As usual, she thought grudgingly. He'd been right a lot today.

Now they could hear voices as well, male voices. Instinctively Brad and Kristen flattened their backs as close as possible to the trunk of the tree, and Kristen quickly drew her knees up and covered her tennis shoes with the skirt of her dress.

Soon the voices became audible.

"… traded duty with Reggie Dawkins. 'Course, when I agreed to it, I had no idea I'd be tramping around the cursed countryside. Blast Reggie, anyway."

"Don't blame him," came another voice, which, like the first, had a distinct British accent; not a cockney dialect, but more refined. "I'd rather not be here either. I was invited to take tea with Miss Lucy Westcott, and I'd much rather be sitting in her comfortable parlor eating tea cakes than jaunting around this god-forsaken forest with you."

The footsteps stopped, and as best Kristen could guess, the two men—and she assumed it was only these two—were about fifteen yards away.

She held her breath.

"Well, then," the first man asked, "what in bloody blazes are we doing 'ere?"

"Followin' orders, that's what."

Brad turned his head to look at the two men, trying to see between the leaves of the shrub that hid them.

"What orders?" the other man asked. "What are we supposed t'be doin', anyway?"

"General Howe's getting' a mite anxious and testy about this attack. He thinks someone might be tryin' to tip off Washington and the colonials."

"Who?"

"Well, if he knew that, he'd put a stop to it, now, wouldn't he?"

"So what are we out here t'do, then? If they want to stop someone from leaving Philadelphia and tip off the Yanks, they'd just keep an eye out on all the roads leaving the city. We're out here in the middle of nowhere. If we see someone, they've already gotten out of the city."

"Precisely. Anyone wantin' to get back *in* is to be stopped and questioned. To find out where they've been, an' all that."

"I'nt that a little back'ards? If they've already been out, and they were carrying word to them Yanks, then they already done it, now, hadn't they?"

"Yeah, but at least we'd know where the leak's coming from and who's spilling' the beans, so to speak. And you can bet General Howe would know how to deal with 'em."

"Well, there ain't nobody out here so far, and I ain't too keen on going any farther. You heard what those dimwitted

Yank deserters said earlier, didn't you? There's some sort of wild animals out in these woods."

"Ah, it was probably just a house cat howling for a friend. But you're right, I'm not lookin' to go further either if I don't have to. It's comin' on dark now, as it is. Let's go back and catch up with Charlie and Tom. They probably ain't seen anything, either, but at least we can all say we patrolled the road, and then spend the rest of our watch nearer to town."

There were footsteps on the rough dirt road, and Brad and Kristen were silent until the sounds had faded completely. Only then did Brad dare to lean out from where they'd been sitting at the base of the tree and look through the shrubbery.

"I think they're gone," he said quietly. He got to his feet and helped his sister up. Motioning for Kristen to stay put, he stepped silently around the shrub to the road.

"Clear," he said.

Kristen too stepped around the bushes, carrying both their packs.

"Well, that sucks," she said. "Howe suspects there might be a leak. I wouldn't want to be Rebecca's mom if he finds out who it is."

"I know, but truthfully, I'd be surprised if she was the only one who's giving intel to the Americans from within Philadelphia; I'm sure there's a whole network of patriots doing what they can to thwart the British. But the takeaway here, the part that we need to be concerned with, is that Howe's monitoring the roads to see not only who tries to get out of the city, but who tries to get back in."

"So? Your friend Mary the Messenger has a magic pass, remember?" Kristen paused to brush the dirt and leaves from her dress. "It's a Golden Ticket back to Wonka-ville. Or, in this case, Philadelphia."

Brad took her by the shoulders, forcing her to look at him. "You're not getting it. Yes, Rebecca has a pass to be outside the city. But General Howe thinks there might be a mole at CTU."

Kristen smirked. "There's always a mole at CTU."

"—so he's certainly watching who leaves Philadelphia." Brad paused for a second, but Kristen still looked blank.

Sighing, he continued. "And if the mole leaves the city, to deliver a certain message about a certain attack, then eventually…."

Click. The light bulb came on, and Kristen's eyes widened. "Then eventually the mole will have to go *back* to the city."

"Bingo. And guess who, at this very moment, should be heading back toward the city."

"Holy crap, Batman. What are we gonna do?"

"First thing we're gonna do is—warn her."

J. Y. Harris

CHAPTER SIX

With a last glance back down the road where the British soldiers had gone, Brad and Kristen started out in the opposite direction. They were silent, each lost in thought. Her earlier reference to CTU hadn't been an accident; this whole day so far had been like a colonial version of the TV show *24*. Spies, turncoats, danger, plans that never quite worked out the way they were supposed to without some unexpected wrinkle. Luckily, in this case, it was pretty clear who the major players were: the colonials, or Americans, led by General Washington, and the British Royal Army, under General Sir William Howe. So there wasn't much chance of there being a secret 'mole' in Washington's camp, or a senior officer under Howe working in cahoots with the colonials on the sly. For this reason, she didn't expect to see Major Clark grab another person by the collar and yell "Who are you working for?" in his best Jack Bauer voice.

She glanced over at Brad. So far the two of them had done a pretty decent job of surviving this whole bizarre day. She wouldn't admit it out loud—at least not to him, not today—but they actually made a pretty good team. And they'd done a darn good job of helping to keep history intact. Secret

90

military information to be delivered? Check. Potential spies to throw off track? Check.

The Everhearts had done the job. It was 'Jack Bauer: the Teen Years.' She bet the long-suffering counter-intelligence agent could not have done better than she and Brad had done.

Obviously they weren't the only heroes of the day; they weren't even the main characters in this little drama. Rebecca was the one who took the big risk in delivering the information on the British attack. And Jacob had been instrumental in getting them all where they need to be safely and quickly.

And their work wasn't over yet.

The siblings had walked at least a mile when they saw Jacob and Rebecca heading toward them. Brad and Kris stopped and waited for the other two to catch up.

"Did you miss us?" Rebecca asked teasingly. "We were on our way back to where we'd left you. There was no need for you to come this way."

"What's wrong?" Jacob asked. Not surprisingly, he could tell something was up.

Okay, maybe he's part Jack Bauer, too. He can hunt and track—and he's armed.

"It's the Brits. General Howe suspects he has a leak somewhere, and he's watching the roads around Philadelphia."

Rebecca smiled. "That doesn't concern us. I already delivered my message, and I have a pass, remember? To get flour." She indicated the flour bag, now full, which Jacob was carrying.

"You don't get it," Brad said, just as he'd said to Kristen earlier. "He's looking at everyone—anyone who goes in *or* out of the city."

Clearly, Rebecca didn't understand, just as Kristen hadn't at first, as her brow wrinkled prettily in confusion. "But I've got my flour. That proves that—"

"Brad is right," Jacob cut in. "The bag of flour proves only that you went to the mill. It doesn't prove that's the *only* place you went, or that that's all you did."

"You've been gone all day," Kristen put in. "It can't take ten, twelve hours to go a few miles to a mill for flour. Even if you tell them what Mr. Tyson said, about the river being flooded."

"Then I'll go back to town by another road."

"That won't help. They'll be watching *all* the roads. If you show up now, even with flour, they'll know you've been gone all day. And that's a big red flag."

"A red flag for what? I don't see how my coming back with a sack of flour—even at this hour of the day—how that could affect anything, or make them suspicious. All it means is that I dawdle or that I'm not very efficient. You think they'd try to put me in jail? For that?"

"No," Jacob said, and he put a hand on her arm. "Chances are the British may say or do nothing to you—today. But they would no longer trust your family. At the very least, they could confine your parents to their house, or not allow them to have visitors, that sort of thing."

"And you can forget Howe having meetings in your dining room," Brad added. "You told me your mother sometimes sells baked goods to some of the officers; that would probably stop, too."

Rebecca looked scared. "No, that can't happen! My mother depends on that extra money. I can't let that happen. I can't allow Howe and his men to become suspicious of her. But—you say I can't go back now, when the patrols are there. So what am I going to do? I can't stay gone. I *have* to go back."

"Don't worry," Brad said. "We'll get you back. Somehow."

They were all silent for a moment. This day—this long, interminable day—had looked like it was just about over. The secret spy message had been delivered. Rebecca had gotten her flour. They were literally within two miles of getting her home to Philadelphia.

And now this.

Jacob led them into the trees so they weren't standing in the middle of the road.

"Let's think about this," he said. "Rebecca has to get back into the city. But all the roads are being watched, and people are being stopped as they return."

"Is there a way to get her into the city by some way other than the roads?" Brad asked.

"I'm sure there is," Jacob said, "but we don't have time to make a scouting expedition and check every road into and out of the entire city."

"What about by water?" Kristen asked. "Didn't there used to be—er, I mean, isn't there a river that goes through the town? I don't know what it was called—er, *is* called. Or, what about the Schuykill?"

Jacob shook his head. "Most likely there will be guards along any river or stream large enough to carry a boat."

"Not to mention, we don't have a boat," Rebecca added.

"Yes, there is that," Kristen acknowledged sheepishly.

They were each silent again, thinking.

"Okay, let's go back to Jacob's idea of using simple logic," Brad said finally. "Here's what we know: Rebecca has to get back to the city. But we have to avoid guards. There are guards on the road at each entry point. And we can't use water or any way in other than the roads."

Jacob nodded, and snapped his fingers. "The problem isn't the road. It's the guards. We need to find out how they're doing their job, so we can do ours."

"How do you propose we do that?" Rebecca asked. "Walk up and ask them?"

Jacob smiled. "Something like that."

*   *   *   *   *

"We shouldn't have let him go," Kristen said. "Not without knowing what he was going to do."

Brad and Rebecca looked up from where they sat. The three young people had retreated into the woods as a group of farmers had come along the road on their way back into the city. And not long after Jacob had left them, a couple of officers on horseback had gone past. Luckily the military men had been too busy talking and joking among themselves to look into the trees and see anyone huddled there.

"We couldn't really stop him," the colonial girl said in response to Kristen.

"Besides, if anybody can take care of himself around here, it's Jacob," Brad added.

Kristen sighed. "I hope you're right. It's getting darker by the minute as the sun goes behind the trees."

And Jacob had been gone for quite a while.

They lapsed into silence again, but came alert a few minutes later at the sound of a whistle.

"Here he comes," Rebecca said, peering down the road where the tavern boy should soon appear.

Brad whistled in return and he and the two girls came out of the woods back onto the road.

Rebecca gasped and ran over toward Jacob. "My word! What did they do to you?"

Brad looked dismayed at the appearance of the other boy. "Oh, man, they got a hold of you, didn't they?"

"What? No, I only went to—" Jacob looked down and laughed as comprehension flooded his features. "No, no, the soldiers didn't do this. I did it to myself." He began to brush dirt off his pants and shirt, and straightened his neck-cloth, which had been askew. Finally he used his hands to comb through his disheveled hair and rubbed more dirt off his face.

"You did this to yourself?" Kristen repeated. "What did you do, roll all the way there?"

Brad smiled. "Maybe he climbed a tree and catapulted himself. Hey, now there's an idea."

"What, turn Rebecca into a human cannonball?"

"No, what I was thinking—"

"Stop!" Jacob cut in. "Brad, I think I know what you're thinking, about the tree, and, as crazy as it sounds, why don't we leave that for later, maybe as a fallback plan. But let me tell you what I did and what I think should happen next.

"First, I did make myself dirty and disheveled-looking, trying to look the part I was going to play. I kept to the woods, staying out of sight and going a little ways down that other road, the one that crosses Germantown Road and leads into the city, and then approached it from that direction. And I used this as my prop." He reached into his leather bag and brought out a small flask.

*   *   *   *   *

The young man, unkempt as he was, staggered down the road toward Philadelphia, singing to himself and brandishing his flask.

"Hey there, mates," he called to the two guards on duty. "How goes the war?"

One soldier nudged the other and sneered. "Look at 'im. One of the colony's finest. Bugger off, wastrel."

"Where'd you come from anyway?" the other soldier inquired. He didn't seem as dismissive as his buddy, and used his bayonet to keep the drunken lout at a distance.

"Here, I mean no harm!" the young degenerate protested. "I just been at me friend Jem's house, celebrating the occasion."

"Yeah? What occasion is that?"

"The occasion that we got our hands on some of the good stuff. It be Saturday, be'n't it? That's occasion enough. In these times o' war, a body has to celebrate when he can." The young man hiccupped and stumbled.

"Hey, what you soldiers a-doin' out here anyway? Aren't you s'posed to be protecting the city?"

"And what d'ye think we're doin'?" came the belligerent reply. "We're keepin' drunken sots like you outta town."

"What, you two?" The young man laughed and hiccupped again. "You think you can keep me out of the city? You and what army?" He laughed loudly at his own joke.

One of the soldiers—bayonet-man—advanced on him. "Aye, we can keep the likes of you out. You ain't gettin' past us to pollute the streets of Philadelphy."

"I'll just go by another road, then."

"Not bloody likely. All roads into town is being guarded, and some of the other blokes ain't as polite as we are."

"Why you want to keep respec'ble people like me out of Philadelphia?"

"We's doin' our job. We been told to not let anyone in without a pass."

"An' how do you know I ain't got one?"

"Ha! The likes o' you?" The soldier snorted. "Even if ye got a pass—which I'm bettin' you ain't—we 'as to take you to our cap'n for questioning, and we'll see what 'e has to say."

"Why would I care what he has t' say?"

The soldier got angry that the young lout was questioning him. "He'll have some questions for you, right enough. Ye'll have to tell 'im where ye been, and what your business is here in town. And then he'll decide if he believes you."

"So--" the young man paused to belch—"you're telling me that even if I got a pass, all right and tight and legal-like, I still have to be questioned and I'd be a suspect of some sort? Like some nefarious thief or spy or somethin'?"

Bayonet-man raised his weapon again. "Who said anything about spies? Why you mention that?"

"Well, you did, I expect. You mentioned it. Leastways, you're talking about a body bein' questioned as if they're suspected of doin' something wrong."

"Ah, I ain't wastin' no more time on you, you buggerin' sot. Get movin' down the road, one way or t'other. You ain't passing into town by us."

The young man sneered. "Well, there's more'n one way to skin a cat, so they say. Don't you worry, mates, I'll find my way in. I got a tankard of ale waitin' for me at the Blue Anchor. And I'll be sure to stop and say hello on my way out again."

Timekeepers: A Revolutionary Tale

"Yeah, good luck to ye with that," the soldier said.   He turned his back and the dirty bumpkin turned down Germantown Road, shuffling unsteadily on his feet and singing as he went.

*   *   *   *   *

"Wow," Brad said after Jacob had finished speaking. "Best. Story. Ever!"

"Yes.   Very   Scarlet   Pimpernel,"   Kristen   added approvingly.   At Brad's surprised look, she said, "What?   I read."

Rebecca waved away this nonsense talk.   "All right, so now we know for sure that all roads into the city are being watched, and the soldiers will not only stop, but also question anyone who tries to enter.   That's even worse than we thought."

"Yeah," said Kristen, the glow of Jacob's exciting story fading quickly, "how does that help us?"

The foursome had slipped back into the forest, and were quiet for a moment as another farmer drove a horse-drawn cart down the road.   The cart was filled with fresh-cut lumber.

Jacob finished brushing dirt off his face and clothing, and now that the cart had passed, he answered Kristen's question. "This helps us by telling us exactly what we're dealing with. Two guards on this road—and none too bright, from the look of them."

"You think we can overpower them?" Brad asked uncertainly.   He didn't sound excited at the prospect; violence was certainly not something he would ever look forward to.

"I'm thinking we don't even try."

"Don't even try!" Kristen exclaimed.   "We can't give up! We're so close and we've come so far."

Jacob looked at Kristen, then at Rebecca and Brad.   "I didn't say anything about giving up. My job is to escort Miss Darrow to Philadelphia, and that's by God what I'm going to do."

"So, if we don't overpower the guards, how are we going to get Rebecca past them? Ask them nicely to turn and look the other way?"

Brad nudged his sister. "Let him talk."

Kristen looked down guiltily and was quiet.

Jacob obviously felt a little better now that he had cleaned himself up; he took a deep breath.

"Like I said before, the problem isn't the road—it's the soldiers. All we have to do is clear the soldiers off the road. And we don't need to resort to violence to do it."

Brad snapped his fingers in sudden comprehension. "Of course!" he said. "We don't have to overpower them. All we need is a distraction. We'll just have to lure them away."

"Lure them away?" Kristen repeated. "Does this involve me standing by the road, flashing some leg?"

He gave his sister the Wrinkled Brow. "We're not hitch-hiking."

Kristen put her hands up in an 'I'm just sayin'' attitude. "We *are* talking about guys here. And as the only female who is *not* trying to get smuggled into the city, I figured I was best qualified to do the distracting and the luring. Which I'm more than willing to do, by the way." She let her backpack drop to the ground. "Pardon me for offering my feminine wiles."

"We don't need feminine wiles," Brad insisted

"If you're talking about distracting them," Jacob said, "I don't believe even *your* considerable charm would be able to do that. These louts actually seemed quite intent on doing their jobs. They would certainly not allow themselves to *both* be distracted by a pretty girl."

Brad's eye was caught by Kristen's backpack, and he looked at it speculatively.

"Well, if they want to be good soldiers and follow orders, maybe we should just give them an order to follow."

The three others looked at him questioningly.

"Kris, once again, I believe this mission—should we choose to accept it—will require our special skills."

"Our special what, now? What skills?"

"Skills we brought from home." He looked meaningfully at her pack.

"Ooo-kay," she replied. "I have no idea what you have in mind, but whatever it is, I'm in."

"Wait," Rebecca broke in. "What are you thinking? I'd like to help."

Brad smiled at her. "You can't help with this. You'll be busy sneaking into the city. With Jacob's assistance, I hope."

Jacob raised his brows. "Without question," he replied. "What is your plan?"

Brad held up a hand. "Give me a minute to confer with my associate and I'll get right back to you on that."

He drew Kristen aside and led her a few yards away.

"Did you say you had the PSP in your backpack?"

She nodded. "Why? We gonna show those guards how to build something in Farm City? Let 'em create characters in Realm of Warriors?"

"Not exactly. Have you been playing Modern Marksman?"

"Not really. That's more your thing than mine. Why?"

"Because I think we can use that. Get me the game, please."

Kristen fished the portable game system out of her bag and handed it to him.

"Thanks. Go back and keep them company for a few minutes. I'm going to find what I'm looking for, but I need to be out of earshot."

Brad rejoined them a few minutes later and Kristen could see the PSP console was in his large jacket pocket.

"Okay," he said, "I think we're set."

"What's the plan?" Jacob asked again.

Dang, Kristen thought. *So now we're at the point at which all this cloak-and-dagger stuff is no big deal, something we do every day on a regular basis.* Rebecca had carried a message with secret information, which could have gotten her and her family charged with treason, with who-knows-what as a punishment. Jacob works at what is most likely an American spy headquarters. He can disappear and move silently through the forest as well as any native. And he created a disguise out of thin air (and brown dirt) to effect a covert reconnaissance mission, and brought in vital information. And now she and Brad were about to use twenty-first century technology to outwit the enemy.

For the second time that day.

And it was all beginning to seem like old hat. In the space of less than a day, they had all gotten so comfortable with such clandestine actions that by now it seemed perfectly ordinary to ask "What's the plan?"

So, Brad told them the plan.

"Kristen and I will go ahead, out of sight, to the road that leads directly into Philly—er, Philadelphia, once it crosses this one, Germantown. At the same time, you two make your way, on the other side of the road, to hide as close to the guards as you can without being seen."

They all nodded, looking very much, Kris thought, like football players in a huddle, listening as the quarterback outlined his plays.

"Then when we're both in position, I'll--er, well... you may hear something that sounds alarming, but don't worry, it's just Kristen and me, so don't panic. If this works, the two soldiers will move away from their post, away from where the two of you will be hiding, and you should be able to slip quietly into the city.

"Well, that's how I envision it working, anyway," he finished, sounding a little embarrassed. "But if anyone else has another idea…."

"No, that sounds good," Jacob said. "I think you're right in drawing the guards away and fooling them. This way they won't raise an alarm of any sort, as they'll have no reason to think anyone got past them."

Timekeepers: A Revolutionary Tale

"And they wouldn't dare tell anyone if they did," Rebecca said. "They'd be too embarrassed and fearful of punishment."

"Um, I have a question," Kristen spoke up. She turned to Jacob. "I hope you're just going to escort Miss Flour-Power here to the entrance of the city and then leave, right? Otherwise, how are you going to get back out? Those guards won't be gone long—maybe just a few minutes."

"I won't let him come inside with me," Rebecca said. "I know that he—that all of you—have risked a lot in helping me, and I won't let him risk his safety any farther." She looked pointedly at Jacob. "Please don't argue with me; once I'm past the guards, I'll be fine."

"But where will you go?" Brad asked. "For all we know, the British have someone watching your mother's house. If you show up now, they'll wonder where you've been all day."

"I'll go to my friend's house, where I've been living," she replied. "I don't normally spend all day there, but it's not impossible that I would. She and her family would gladly vouch for the fact that I arrived there at—oh, noon, at the latest."

"I wish we knew when they put the guards out to watch everyone who went in and out," Jacob said. "If we knew that, Rebecca could say she got back to the city before that hour. As it is, she could still get questioned, if the guards had been in place since morning. The guards on duty would be questioned too, maybe even asked to identify you."

She shrugged. "There's nothing we can do about that now. I left early this morning, and would probably have been back by eleven o'clock, noon at the latest. I'll go to my friends, and if anyone asks, I'll say I was taken ill and slept the afternoon away."

"Taken ill? Will anyone believe that?"

"I do sometimes get very strong headaches. Not very often, thankfully, but it's something my family and friends know about me, so they'll believe it easily enough."

"Well, if they believe it, let's hope they can convince the Brits to believe it too," Brad said.

"So, are we ready then?" Jacob asked. "The sun dips lower by the minute."

"Yes, I guess we'd best get on with it."

The four teens stood looking at each other, suddenly aware that it was time to say goodbye. They also knew it was most likely to be goodbye forever; Jacob and Rebecca may each think it conceivable they may one day run into the others again, either in Philadelphia, or at the tavern, or somewhere on the road in between.

But Kristen and Brad knew that would never happen. They knew that, to the two colonials, the Everhearts would become just a memory of paths crossed. An adventure involving strangers who appeared (literally) out of nowhere, and were never to be seen again.

To Brad and Kristen, the other two would become memories as well, but the difference was that they *knew* their paths would never cross again. Jacob and Rebecca would become not just history, in the sense of names in a text book, but memories as well, of an adventure shared and company enjoyed.

That is, if they ever got home again.

At the moment, Rebecca was the one saying goodbye. If this plan worked, she would slip into Philadelphia and rejoin her family. Jacob would come back and try to meet up with the siblings again, hopefully without being seen.

Rebecca allowed each boy to take her hand in farewell, and then surprised Kristen by hugging her.

"I don't know why you've been calling me those silly names, like Pie-Girl, or Flour-Girl, or what-have-you, but you're a very good person, Kristen Everheart. I'll always remember what you've done for me this day."

Kristen suddenly found it difficult to speak. "Well," she said over the lump in her throat, "we'll make sure that people remember what *you* did this day, too. It was very courageous."

Timekeepers: A Revolutionary Tale

Jacob cleared his throat to remind them that they were out of time. Ever the practical one, Kristen thought. Well, that's okay; if Jacob Tyson ever stepped through the mysterious portal of fog and landed in her and Brad's world, *they* would be the practiced ones who could navigate the surroundings with ease. But this was *his* time, and he knew what he was doing.

All too soon, there was nothing else to do but go. Brad took Kristen's arm and pulled her farther into the woods. Jacob led Rebecca across the road and into the trees on the other side.

"Are you sure you know what you're doing?" Kris asked her brother.

"Pretty much," he replied. "Sort of. I hope."

"Well, nothing like being confident. Ow! Stupid root! This is getting tricky, now that the woods are getting so much darker. I have a flashlight, though. Should we use it?"

"Not yet. Too dangerous. Somebody might see."

"Yeah, like us, maybe? Heaven forbid we should be able to see where we're walking."

"It's not that bad; your eyes should have adjusted. Don't try to look too far ahead; just look immediately in front of you."

"Yeah, I guess that's better."

"Okay," Brad whispered. "Right up here is where the other road comes in and crosses Germantown, I'm pretty sure it's Frankford Road, and goes straight south, into Philly. And there are the guards. Just keep quiet and step carefully. We've got to go down Frankford a little bit, away from the city."

She stayed behind Brad and watched where she put her feet. On the right they were approaching where the soldiers stood, pacing their little fiefdom at the intersection of the two roads. Soon she could hear the murmur of their voices, and an occasional laugh.

The other side of the road was not heavily wooded; there were a few trees, but mainly tall grass and scrub bushes not even waist high.

Jacob and Rebecca would have their work cut out for them to advance in that landscape. That's okay, though; by the time Brad and I make our way up Frankford, out of sight, they should definitely be in position.

She and Brad walked parallel to Frankford Road, just until they were out of sight of the crossroads and the soldiers. With the trees and the oncoming gloom and all, that wasn't too difficult to accomplish.

"Okay," Brad said. "Are you ready?"

"I guess so. Let's just hope Jacob and Rebecca are ready."

"Don't worry about them. Once they hear the commotion, and the guards do their thing, Jacob won't hesitate."

"You're right. Okay, let's get this show on the road."

Brad took the game system out of his pocket.

"Yes. Let's."

CHAPTER SEVEN

Forty yards away, Jacob and Rebecca were crouched amid the tall grass and weeds near the intersection of the two roads. It had been slow going, but luckily the two soldiers had kept up a steady conversation between themselves, so they didn't hear every rustle of brush around them. Unfortunately, some of their conversation consisted of bawdy jokes and raw language, and Jacob had to clench his jaw at the thought of Miss Darrow's ears being sullied in such a way.

But they had gotten to within fifteen yards of the road, and this was as close as he dared go. When the time came, he was ready to run with Miss Darrow—to pull her, if necessary—out of the weeds and then down Frankford Road and into the city.

Jacob thought back to his little performance earlier, when, as he was supposedly drunk and arguing with the guards, he had been looking past them into Philadelphia.

A short way past the intersection where the guards stood, about thirty yards or so, was the first building. It didn't look like a house; perhaps it was a barn or storage shed. The opposite side of the road had a small fence, beyond which were a couple of chicken coops and a privy. If worse came to worst, he could boost Miss Darrow over the fence and into that yard and she would be able to walk unobtrusively out on the other side, as if she'd come from the house.

Next to him in the tall grass, the girl from Philadelphia looked calm. For someone who had walked countless miles since early morning to deliver urgent news to the Continental Army, and who was now waiting to sneak, like a thief, back into her own city under cover of darkness, she looked remarkably at ease. Alert and ready, yes, but still calm.

They had been in position for close to twenty minutes, stretched out uncomfortably on their stomachs on the hard ground. Jacob had just started to wonder if something had happened to prevent Brad and Kristen Everheart from carrying out their plan.

"You there!"

The rough voice rang out in the deepening dusk. The two young people hiding in the tall grass stiffened. Had they been discovered after all?

"Soldier, you better snap to attention when I'm talking to you!"

Aha.

The two guards nearly dropped their muskets in surprise, but they did indeed snap to attention.

The voice, the booming, unmistakable voice of authority, had come from along Frankford Road, rather than inside the city. It took a moment, but finally the soldiers seemed to figure out precisely in which direction they should direct their attention.

"New orders have just come in. Come forward and report!"

The guards looked at each other uncertainly.

"You heard the captain. Come forward!"

That second voice was Brad's, Jacob knew; he had no idea who the first one belonged to, but he knew this was his signal. He found Rebecca's hand and squeezed it, signaling her to be ready.

The two British soldiers, however, didn't move.

"Captain 'oo?" one of the startled soldiers hissed to the other. "No captain or any other officer has left the city that I knows of."

"Cor, I don't know. 'Less they went out afore we came on duty. Or what if they left the city by some other road, and are just returning this way?"

The voice came again, barking, "Do I have to repeat myself, soldier?"

At that, the two British guards stepped smartly forward. Jacob wondered briefly where they thought they were going, but it didn't really matter.

As long as they were gone.

"Incoming RPG! Load those anti-missile—"

Even though the sentence was cut off suddenly, the urgency of that authoritative voice was unmistakable. The soldiers quickened their pace to a quit trot.

"This way, soldiers!" Brad's voice again. "Double-time!"

Finally, as the soldiers made their way in the opposite direction, Jacob felt it was safe for him and Rebecca to scramble up from their position, knowing that the sounds of the soldiers' feet on the road would cover any sounds they might make. He had Rebecca's flour sack in one hand, and the other had taken hold of her wrist. Once they reached the road, they quickened their pace, hurrying as quickly—and quietly—as possible toward the buildings ahead.

Rebecca's foot got caught in the hem of her gown. If she'd had her hands free, she would have held the gown up a bit to prevent just such an occurrence, but with Jacob holding her wrist, this wasn't possible.

When she faltered, he shot out his other hand to steady her, then they continued forward. His fingers loosened on her wrist and slipped down to her hand.

Finally, they reached the small fence he'd seen earlier. Although they could hear muted sounds and voices from the city street ahead, nobody was in the yard, and the house to which the yard belonged was dark.

"I'll get you over the fence," Jacob said in a low voice. "Then you can go around the house to the cross street."

She nodded, barely visible in the deepening shadows. "Willow Street, I'm familiar with it. I'll be fine. Thank you, Jacob. You're a real gentleman."

He smiled, a bit crookedly. "Only when I have to be. If circumstances were different, who knows what I might attempt with such a fair young lady?"

She smiled, too, and plucked a piece of grass out of his hair. "If circumstances were different, who knows what I might allow such a handsome young man?"

Jacob looked surprised, and then laughed. "Next time you have a pass to travel outside the city, you know where to find me. I promise you'll get a good meal, and a very proper, gentlemanly escort back to the city after you've eaten it."

"Well, where's the incentive in that?" she asked, laughing even as she spoke.

He looked as if he were about to say something, and then thought better of it. "Come on, I'll boost you over the fence."

Jacob lifted her so that she was sitting on the top rail of the split-rail fence. Rebecca then swung her legs over to the other side and hopped down. She took the flour sack from him.

He caught her hand. "Farewell, message-carrier." He brought her hand to his lips and kissed the back of her fingers. Then he turned her hand and brought her palm up to his lips.

A dog barked not far away, and Rebecca jumped. She pulled her hand back and clutched the flour sack with both hands.

"Goodbye, Jacob," she said in a hushed, breathless voice. "Stay safe."

She turned and hurried through the yard toward the street.

Jacob stood still for a moment, listening to be sure no alarm was raised or disturbance created. When all remained quiet, he melted back into the shadows and made his way along the side of the road back toward the crossroads of Germantown and Frankford Roads.

As he approached the intersection, he could just make out two forms coming toward him along Frankford Road. Luckily, the two soldiers were preoccupied with their own thoughts and not looking for movement in the nearby weeds. Or listening for it, for that matter.

"What the 'ell d'ye think that was?" one asked, the one who had held his bayonet on Jacob earlier.

"I dunno," the other replied. "But I feel a proper fool for having marched down the road after it, whatever it was."

"And march smartly, too, no less. That was some of me best marchin', that was. And for what? There was nobody there!"

"Well, I know I heard them voices, and you did too, no denyin'."

"Yeah, but 'oo's gonna believe us? 'Oo's gonna believe them voices was real, when there warn't nobody there?"

"Nobody, that's 'oo. Ain't nobody gonna believe it, cuz we ain't gonna tell anyone."

"Not tell—"

"Shh. Keep your voice down. It'll be time for our relief to come soon, and I want nothin' more than to get to my dinner and ale, without any fuss or commotion. And that ain't gonna 'appen if we start talkin' about voices in the woods, and phantom orders."

"But—"

"But nothing'! You want to be questioned and reamed out half the night? You want the Cap'n to know we stepped away from our appointed post and left it unguarded as we went chasin' down the road after shadows?"

"Well, no, the Cap'n'd skin our 'ides."

"Exactly. Now, there's no 'arm done—all's right and tight here, ain't it? Nobody ever has to know what just 'appened, or what we just done. Got it?"

"Yus, I got it. And I ain't gonna let go of it, neither. Like you say, no harm done, and nobody seen it. Guess I'm with you, and I'd just as soon pretend it never 'appened."

"Good, we're agreed: it never 'appened. Now, let's just take a moment to reflect, and start with the forgettin'." He let out a breath. "So, what d'ye think we'll be 'aving for our supper?"

Jacob had heard enough. He began inching his way slowly through the brush away from the road crossing.

Suddenly, he stopped. Someone was approaching—he could feel it. Faint vibrations in the ground beneath him told him so. Lifting his head, he pinpointed the source of the sensation: Frankford Road. A horse—no, two horses.

A few seconds later, the two soldiers heard the horses too. They immediately straightened up and took up an official pose. Almost like real soldiers, Jacob thought wryly.

The horses came into view: one rider was a man, the other a woman, the skirt of her habit draped gracefully over the horse's flank as she rode sidesaddle. The riders calmly approached the two soldiers.

Jacob knew that the sound of the clopping hooves and the soldiers' attention being drawn to the riders would easily cover any slight rustling of grass he caused. But, to be safe, he stayed put. Just for the moment.

The man on horseback spoke confidently to the soldiers, and produced a paper from inside his coat; no doubt one of the travelling passes Jacob had heard so much about.

To their credit, the soldiers looked soldierly, and at least seemed as if they knew what they were doing. One of them held the pass up to look at it in the fading light, and Jacob could hear him question the man. Apparently the pass indicated that the two riders were acquainted with a Major Lorne, whom they were expecting to meet in the city. The sentries had not seen anyone by that name, but since the riders had the appropriate documentation, they soon let the man and woman pass.

Timekeepers: A Revolutionary Tale

As the horses made their way into the city of Philadelphia, no doubt smelling the nice warm stables waiting for them ahead, Jacob continued his slow, steady retreat through the tall weeds.

Once he got far enough away from the road crossing, where the trees became more plentiful, Jacob felt safe enough to get to his feet and make his way along the treeline.

He started as there was a sudden commotion in the brush next to him; a mouse or squirrel, perhaps? Or maybe a possum, waking to begin its nocturnal wanderings. Unlike most animals, this didn't continue to make noise; it was abruptly quiet.

Whatever it was, Jacob couldn't see it. It was certainly nothing large, so it presented no threat to him.

Finally, after he'd gone almost a mile or so along Germantown Road, he could barely make out two figures up ahead, standing in the road. Jacob gave the whistle he'd used earlier, and after a few seconds, he heard another whistle in reply. It wasn't the one Brad had used earlier, the fake bird call; this was just a human-sounding whistle, which Jacob thought was odd.

Well, it had been a long day, and, whistle or no whistle, he was looking forward to a mug of warm wine and a hearty potato. Like a horse sensing its stable, he could almost smell the tasty dinner ahead of him. It had no doubt been a long day for the Everheart siblings as well, and if they agreed to join him at the tavern, so much the better.

Suddenly Jacob tensed. He had let his mind wander for a moment as he made his way up the road, but now he realized that rather than his two young friends, the figures he saw ahead were both tall, and both male.

Jacob stopped. What an idiot he'd been! Contrary to his training, contrary to his common sense, contrary to everything he'd ever practiced, he'd let his guard down, and this was where it had led him. Thinking quickly, he knew the strangers had obviously seen him; there was nothing for it now but to approach them openly.

He cursed under his breath. His mistake was inexcusable, and, worse, was now potentially dangerous. Was this the reason Brad's whistle had been different? Had he been trying to warn Jacob about something amiss?

In the deepening dusk, Jacob saw one of the figures—a soldier, he saw now—lift something, and knew that the 'something' was a musket, leveled right at him. At this distance he was well within range for reasonable accuracy from a good marksman.

Worse, Jacob could now see the form of a horse in the shadows near the trees; even if he ran, unless he stuck to the woods, he'd be easily overtaken.

Since he was no longer advancing toward them, one of the soldiers—the one with the Brown Bess—started walking toward Jacob.

"Who are you?" he asked.

"Just a wayfarer travelling peaceably along the road," Jacob answered. "And who might you be?"

"I'm a soldier on the King's business. Do you have any paperwork, or a pass to be on the road?"

"I didn't know I needed such. I'm a free person travelling on open road."

"Travellers to or from Philadelphia need a pass to cross its border. In or out." This officer was obviously not one to be trifled with. His crisp, matter-of-fact manner said he would brook no nonsense.

"There's the answer to the confusion, then," Jacob said with an easy smile. "I'm not from Philadelphia. Nor, obviously, am I headed that way. I come from the Frankford Road."

"And where are you headed?"

Jacob was perfectly willing to answer some questions and comply with someone who was just doing his job, but this officer was a little too sharp for comfort.

For Jacob's comfort, certainly.

He didn't want to antagonize the officer. This one was of quite a different stamp from the two bumbling slackers he'd encountered guarding the road into Philadelphia.

Yes, this one was definitely sharp. And that was dangerous.

In answer to the question, Jacob replied, "I'm heading toward the Wheel Pump Tavern on the King's Highway. Do you know it? I've been on the road a good part of the day, and am looking forward to a meal and a bed."

"Yes, I know the place," the redcoat replied, eying Jacob. "Their biscuits are very good, and their stew is always tasty. Where are you coming from on the Frankford Road?"

Oh, he's good, Jacob thought. First agreeing with his statement, drawing him into casual conversation, and then the sudden change of subject, obviously trying to catch him off-guard.

Jacob, however, didn't fall into the trap. He'd been around enough British soldiers to know that you should never, ever, let down your guard. You have a part to play—in his case, on this particular evening, the innocent bumpkin traversing the countryside—and you have to play it for all you're worth. You have to live it, breathe it, own it, as Major Clark had told him countless times. Never show doubt or hesitation. Those are the telltale signs of a liar.

Or, a very poor spy.

Without hesitation, Jacob answered the soldier's question. "I've been visiting a friend who lives near Frankford."

"And where are you headed?"

"I told you, the tavern on the King's Highway."

"Is that your final destination, or are you just stopping there?"

"If you must know, I'm hoping to get a job there. I hear they may need someone to clear tables and mop floors."

The officer had advanced closer to Jacob as they spoke, and Jacob knew that if he bolted now, he'd be both shot at and chased on horseback. Even if he ran through the forest he didn't know how far he'd get; if he managed to make an escape, the local British regiments would be alerted to look for him for having fled questioning.

No, even though he wasn't doing anything wrong, he'd do better to answer a few questions and see if he could wiggle out of this on his own. It was his own fault he was in this mess; he sure as blazes wasn't going to lead the British toward anyone else while trying to get out of it.

"Yes, a steady job is always a good thing," the officer said dryly. He was still advancing on Jacob, slowly, casually, as if they were just two people who'd stopped to chat.

Jacob was aware that the second soldier had circled widely around, and was now standing behind him.

Cutting off his retreat.

On one hand, that made this easier for Jacob, as now, with one soldier in front of him, and another behind him, he would have to bolt either to the right or left; either way would take him right into the woods.

The woods he knew like the back of his hand.

"I know where you've been," the officer said.

"Of course you do. I just told you where I've been."

"No. I know where you've really been."

"So do I. I know where I've really been."

"You've just come from Philadelphia."

It was a statement; a confident one, certainly, but Jacob knew he was just guessing.

Jacob laughed. "Now, I can see where you might think that, with this road leading into and out of the city, and all. But I'm telling you, I came down the Frankford Road. Besides, how could I have been in Philadelphia? You just told me people need a pass to get in or out, and I ain't got one."

The officer seemed to consider this. He made a hand gesture, and from behind him, Jacob heard a flint struck. The scene brightened as the soldier behind him obviously lit a torch.

Jacob hadn't realized the redcoat was that close behind him, but then, he'd felt it more important to keep his attention on the officer in front of him.

Now, with both soldiers so close, Jacob knew he was fairly caught. He hadn't wanted to run before, as that would have aroused suspicions which could possibly have been avoided.

But now, he might not get the chance at all. Running would lead them to believe that he had something to hide.

And he didn't.

At least, not as far as the British soldiers were concerned. There was no way they could prove he'd been in Philadelphia, or that he hadn't, in fact, come down the Frankford Road.

Even the two redcoat dolts who were patrolling the entrance into the city would swear he hadn't been there.

No, the officer had no reason to hold him, Jacob knew.

The question was, how long would it be before the officer knew it?

The soldier raised his musket away from Jacob and slung it by its strap over his shoulder. His eyes, however, were still on Jacob as he held his hand out.

"Torch, please."

The soldier handed the officer the torch. The flame caused shadows on the officer's face to dance.

"It appears there's not much more we can learn at the moment," he said in his clipped British accent, and Jacob exhaled a breath he hadn't realized he'd been holding.

Then the officer said, "Take him, sergeant. Bind him to a tree until we can get him to the garrison for more questioning."

"Hey!" Before Jacob could react, his arms were seized from behind and held fast. "What're you doing?" he protested. "I told you where I been. You have no reason to detain me. What more do you want?"

"I want the truth. We know someone's leaking information and carrying it to the colonials, and we want to know who, and how."

"I don't have any information. Like I said, I'm just making my way to the Wheel Pump Tavern."

"We'll see about that. Sergeant, once you tie him to the tree, search him. I want to see everything he's carrying."

"Yes sir, Cap'n Pendragon."

Jacob made a mental inventory of what was in his pockets. He was always very careful, and was glad to know that nothing he carried could either identify or incriminate him.

The sergeant led Jacob off the road—and none too gently, either--and put him with his back to a tree; he then bound his hands behind him, around the trunk. He also wrapped a rope around Jacob's ankles and tied that behind the tree as well.

Jacob muttered an oath. *Looks like I should've run when I had the chance. But who knew I'd run across such a stickler of an officer?*

Well, he'd been in worse spots than this. And gotten out of them. Jacob was just glad the Everhearts weren't with him. It was bad enough to find himself in such a ridiculous—and embarrassing—situation. And on top of that, to now have to get himself out of it.

It was good he didn't have to worry about *them* as well. With luck, Brad and Kristen were deep into the forest somewhere, on their way to meet—well, whoever they're supposed to meet.

Those are two strange birds, he told himself.

CHAPTER EIGHT

Jacob idly watched as the two soldiers went about their business. The officer—Captain Pendragon—stowed his musket in the saddle of his horse and pulled out a paper from one of the saddlebags. The other one, the sergeant, tried not to look useless.

"Pssst!"

Jacob's head snapped up with alertness, his eyes darting left and right.

"Pssst! Behind you, but don't turn your head."

He kept still.

"It's me, Kris. Kristen," said the low voice from right behind the trunk to which he was tied. The two British soldiers were quite a ways in front of him; as long as he didn't make noise or try to move, Jacob didn't think they'd pay any attention to him or otherwise bother with him.

He put his head down and to the side.

"What are you doing here? Get away, the both of you."

"No way. We're Americans. We don't leave our friends behind."

"Look, I have no idea what that means, although it sounds nice. But I'll be fine. I've got a plan."

"Yeah? What's your plan?"

"Well, actually… My only plan is to try to come up with a plan. But I will."

Jacob felt tugging on the rope binding his wrists behind him. Suddenly it went slack.

"Now, don't move," Kristen whispered. "Pretend the ropes are still in place. You'll know when to make your move."

"When?"

"You'll know it when it happens. It'll be very startling, but don't hesitate. Just run into the forest to your right. That's important—to your right. Capiche?"

"What?"

"You got it?"

"Got what?"

He heard a sigh. "Do you understand?"

"Oh. Yes, I understand. Run to the right."

"Bingo. Now wait for the signal."

A slight rustle of bushes, and he knew she was gone.

Jacob turned his attention back to the Redcoats. The torch had been stuck into a convenient rabbit hole at the edge of the road, giving enough light for the two soldiers to go about their business.

Captain Pendragon's uniform had the buff facings of the 22nd Regiment. Last Jacob had heard, that regiment had been up near New York City. Pendragon must be travelling to Philadelphia for a reason. And taking a roundabout way to get there. The captain was still perusing the paper he'd taken out of his saddlebag.

The sergeant was inspecting the knife he'd taken from Jacob earlier, before he'd tied him up. The man looked over at the captive and grinned smugly. He used the point of Jacob's knife to clear dirt from underneath his gritty fingernails.

Jacob's arms ached to smack that satisfied look off his ugly face. Well, he might not get a chance to do that, once the 'signal'—whatever it was—finally came. But if the opportunity presented itself….

Timekeepers: A Revolutionary Tale

The British captain folded the paper he'd been looking at and opened his saddlebag to return it.

Suddenly the air seemed to explode with a deafening noise. A bright light appeared from above, from high up in the trees.

In front of him, Jacob saw the two soldiers seemingly frozen in a circle of white light, both looking up in confusion. The sergeant dropped Jacob's knife, and Captain Pendragon tucked the folded paper into the pocket of his saddlebag with one hand, even while his gaze was drawn upward.

The thunderous sound came again in another bone-rattling explosion. The captain's horse danced and sidestepped nervously, snorting in confusion.

This must be it, Jacob thought. *This must be the signal. If it's not, then it's some unbelievable coincidence, but in either case, it's about as good of a distraction as I'm likely to get.*

He kicked off the rope that lay slack around his ankles. The other rope, the one that had bound his wrists behind the tree trunk, he stuffed into his coat pocket. Good rope was expensive; he could always use an extra length.

Jacob surged forward. He knew the plan was for him to dive to the right and run, but he had something to do first.

He scooped up the knife—his knife—from where that clod of a sergeant had dropped it. Then, in one fluid movement, Jacob grabbed the paper that Captain Pendragon had tried to stow back in the saddlebag. The sheet was only half inside the pocket of the leather bag, with one corner conveniently ripe for plucking; the horse's nervous dancing had probably kept it from falling into place where it belonged. Jacob also slipped the horse's rein from around the low shrub over which it had been tossed, and slapped the animal's rump.

What with the sudden noise and confusion, the horse needed no further urging to bolt.

Only then did Jacob run in the direction in which he'd been instructed to go.

As he ducked into the trees, Jacob heard a commotion behind him. He heard a shout, and the sergeant's voice bleating something about an 'escape.' The impulsive seconds he'd spent retrieving his knife and the Captain's paper had obviously cost him dearly, as it had also alerted the soldiers to his activity. The Brits would surely be hot on his heels.

However, as he dodged his way through the trees, Jacob became aware there were no sounds of pursuit behind him. He stopped and looked back.

The strange noise had stopped, and as he stood there and watched, the white circle of light from above disappeared as suddenly as it had appeared, leaving the forest and road darker than ever. In the distance—in the opposite direction from where he was, and to the left of where he'd been tied to the tree—he heard a commotion in the forest, and raised voices.

Either Kristen or Brad had drawn off the soldiers in that direction, pretending to be him. Where the other sibling was— and what that bright light and thunderous noise had been—he didn't know.

Jacob resumed his trek in the direction he'd been going, stealthily, quietly, but at a more leisurely pace.

After a while he stopped, and gave the bird whistle signal. It was answered immediately from not very far away, and seconds later he saw Brad Everheart approach in the deepening gloom.

"Glad you're okay," Brad said, slapping him on the shoulder. "You threw us for a loop back there, when you didn't run immediately into the woods."

Jacob didn't know what 'loop' Brad was talking about, but he was pretty sure he understood what the other boy meant.

"I'm sorry," he said, "but I had to retrieve a few things from the soldiers."

"What did they take from you?"

"My knife—and my pride. I can't believe I was stupid enough to let them catch me."

"There wasn't much you could've done about that," Brad replied. "Kris and I saw the whole thing from the woods. We tried to get your attention, to let you know the two people you saw weren't us, but we were too far away. I even threw a rock that landed somewhere near you, to try to get your attention."

"Once I discovered they weren't you, I should have bolted."

Brad shook his head. "That would only have guaranteed them coming after you. By stopping and cooperating, you had a fifty-fifty chance that they'd let you go. You had no way of knowing they'd tie you up."

This was all what Jacob had figured, too. His chagrin at walking into the situation was mollified by the fact that, not only did he get away—with some help, of course—but he also managed to get away with a souvenir. He patted the pocket that held the document that Captain Pendragon had been perusing.

He had no idea what it was: it could be a list of garments the captain had sent to the laundry, or a letter from his wife, or something equally innocuous.

On the other hand, it could be a battle map, or a list of troop movements, or suggested supply routes.

Whatever it was, Major Clark would certainly like to see it.

Jacob changed the subject. "Where's Miss Everheart?"

"She should be here soon," Brad replied. He sounded the bird call again.

The two boys were silent for a moment or two, listening, but all they heard were the sounds of the forest. Then, just when Jacob was wondering why Brad wasn't concerned for his sister, and why the two of them had been separated to begin with, he heard a slight rustle of leaves and brush.

He tensed, wondering if, rather than being Kristen, it could be one of the British soldiers approaching. He and Brad hadn't exactly been whispering their conversation just now.

That thought was dispelled, however, when Kristen came into view, disheveled and breathing a bit heavily.

"Boy, that was fun!" she declared, her smile just visible in the darkness.

"What was fun?" Jacob asked.

"Running. It's a little dicey, tearing through the woods—at night—but that's what made it exciting. Hoo!" She let out another breath. "Wicked fun!"

Jacob pointed at her. "So you're the one who led the soldiers away?"

"Yep. They're so far gone in the other direction, they're probably halfway back to where they started from."

"So if you were leading them in the other direction," Jacob said, while pointing to Kristen, "then what were you doing?" And he pointed to Brad with his other hand.

"Me? I provided the distraction."

Jacob's eyebrows rose. "Not the strange light and that awful sound?"

"Yep, that was yours truly."

"But how--?"

Brad clapped him on the shoulder. "You don't want to know. Let's just say it involved reviving my childhood tree-climbing skills and the wonders of an LED flashlight."

Jacob was about to ask another question—like what in heaven's name an LED flashlight was—when Kristen spoke up.

"Look, I know I did a primo job of leading those lobsterbacks into the next zip code, but let's not press our luck by standing here yakking. Let's head back toward the tavern, shall we?"

The boys agreed, and the trio set out together in the appropriate direction.

Jacob fell into step with Kristen. "So you really led the soldiers through the forest?"

"Yeah," she replied. "It would've been easier if I could have seen where I was going; running in this kind of terrain in the dark is *tough*. But if I couldn't see much, neither could they. So I guess it all evened out."

"You must be pretty fast."

She shrugged. "Middle school track champion. Although I would have been faster if I hadn't been wearing this friggin' dress."

Jacob tried not to think about the girl next to him not wearing that dress, or what she would have preferred to be wearing (or not wearing) instead.

"I'm telling you, Kris," Brad said from behind them, "you need to try out for the high school jay-vee track team in the spring. You've got it in you."

"Eh, maybe." To Jacob she said, "Where we come from, we run for sport."

"Really? So you run foot-races? The girls too?"

"Yep, girls too."

"Must be difficult running in those long, heavy skirts."

Kristen flashed him a smile. "I won't get into details of how we run, but let's just say the long skirts are not a problem."

Brad spoke up. "Hey, Jake, I guess everything went okay? Earlier, I mean, with Rebecca."

"Yep, just like you planned. The soldiers went to follow the unexpected orders, and Miss Darrow and I slipped past from Germantown Road and into the city."

"Did you run into anyone on the street?" Kristen asked.

"No, we saw no one. We came up on some buildings—I don't know if they were houses or not—and I left Miss Darrow to slip through a side yard into the cross-street on the other side. I waited a few minutes to be sure she wasn't discovered, but nobody raised an alarm or called out. All was quiet."

"Well, I guess no news is good news," she replied.

Brad nodded in the deepening dusk. "And I guess that since we have no way of finding out exactly what happened with her—if she got to her friend's house, if she'll be questioned—there's nothing for us to do except be on our way."

The three young people walked quietly for a moment, and soon came to a road, rougher and not as well travelled as Germantown Road had been. As if by some unspoken agreement, they moved to walk in the grass alongside. It wasn't likely there would be any traffic on this road at night, even though there was a three-quarter moon, but there was no reason to take chances.

Jacob was no doubt thinking of getting back to the tavern; a hot meal, a warm fire, and a comfortable bed awaited him there. Or at least, whatever passed for 'comfortable' in these times, Kristen thought. To her, a colonial bed would probably look like a giant bedspread stuffed with straw. But she'd be glad for a hot meal and a warm fire herself.

And as for a bed... well, there was no point in even thinking about that. Her own bed, with its brightly-colored spread, not to mention the stuffed tiger and giraffe incongruously standing guard together on the matching pillow... that comfort was miles away. Sort of.

She pushed thoughts of it aside... as well as thoughts of the dining-room table, which she would give her right arm to be able to set for dinner—never mind the fact that she normally tried to squirm out of that duty whenever it was her turn to do so. But the thought of doing such a mundane, ordinary task was like gold to her now.

Now... when she felt like she'd never have the chance to do it again.

Be careful what you wish for....

Jacob and Brad had kept up a desultory conversation as they walked. Talking because there was not much else to do, yet not wanting to talk because there was not much to say. Plus, they were all tired. Sure, these colonials were used to walking a lot, but still, dealing with covert agents, sneaking through the forest, tracking soldiers who were AWOL... it sure does wear a body out.

Timekeepers: A Revolutionary Tale

Not to mention tricking people, luring them away from one spot and to another, and sneaking into a city.

Yeah, all in all, it had been a pretty full day.

After they'd walked a couple miles, Jacob said, "It's time to quit following the road. The quickest way for me to get back to the tavern is to go through the forest."

"Yeah," Brad said, looking around. "This is about where we came out of the woods before, when you and Rebecca went to the mill for flour, and Kris and I waited for you."

The three teens entered the forest, with Jacob leading the way in the silvery moonlight. As she had done earlier, Kristen followed immediately behind her brother, practically on his heels, so she wouldn't trip in the uneven, leaf-strewn ground.

Funny how she'd had no trouble running hell-for-leather through the forest earlier, but now she was being careful where she stepped. And earlier she'd complained to her brother about this very thing.

What a difference an hour makes. Not to mention the adrenaline rush of a good plan executed in the dark.

Now that the adrenaline was no longer pumping through her veins, Kristen's spirits were sinking by the minute. On one hand, she expected—she knew—that she and Brad would somehow find their way back to their own time. She didn't know—didn't care—if this 'knowing' came from real conviction, a knowledge deep in her soul, like a hardwired message from the cosmos... or if she believed it simply because she had to, for sanity's sake. Because the alternative was too awful to contemplate.

Her and Brad's being stuck in this time anomaly was bad enough—no TV, no cars, no heat, no family or friends...or cellphones with which to call them—but worst of all, the thing that upset her the most was: her parents.

If necessary, Kris knew that she and Brad could survive in this time period. It's not like they could change things, or alter the circumstances or technology of the eighteenth century, so they'd adapt to it, if only because they had to, had no other choice. It wouldn't be fun, and they wouldn't enjoy it or choose it, but they *could* do it.

But the thought of what their parents would go through—are probably going through right now…. She hated to think of it. She and Brad had left that morning—a Saturday, when they usually both slept in, like most lazy kids their age—to go to a local park for an historical re-enactment.

They were teenagers, two healthy, intelligent, capable teenagers. The fact that two teens could both disappear into thin air—or, in this case, fog—was probably going to be the most perplexing thing of all. One person, especially a child, would be one thing; he or she could wander off or be lured away. Even a lone teenager could be believed: a secret plan to meet a friend, or perhaps even run away for some ridiculous reason.

But *two* teens? That never happens.

All Kristen knew was that her mom and dad would be worried to death, and would move heaven and earth to find them.

For their sake, she didn't want to contemplate the notion that she and Brad would never get home. It was just not an option that she would consider.

Cutting into her gloomy thoughts, Brad said "Watch out for this—"

Whack!

"—branch."

Just like in a cartoon, she thought wryly.

"Thanks," she said. "That warning helped. What's another tear in this skirt, anyway?"

"Sorry," he said. "I had already stepped past the branch when I saw it."

"You two all right back here?" Jacob asked, stopping to turn back to them.

"We'll be fine. Just a bit of a wardrobe malfunction."

Even in the moonlight Kristen could see Jacob's confusion.

"It's nothing," she assured him.

"Still, I apologize. Traipsing through the forest is not new to me, even at night. I forget that others aren't as used to it as I am."

"You're a capable guy," Kristen said. "And that's a good thing. No need to apologize for it."

He smiled, easily visible in the moonlight. "Speaking of capable, you two aren't bad yourselves. You scared those deserters out of spying on General Washington's army, you lured away those soldiers guarding the road into Philadelphia... *and* you provided a distraction for me to get away a while ago." He looked at them shrewdly. "And I'd still like to know why you won't discuss how you did any of those things."

Brad shrugged. "Oh, come on. You must've heard me pretending to be an officer, barking orders at those guys."

"Yes, I heard that. I also heard other voices. Voices that did *not* come from you."

Kristen put her hand on Jacob's shoulder. "We have a saying where we're from: 'I could tell you, but then I'd have to kill you.'"

"What kind of saying is that?"

She shrugged and the three of them started walking again. "I thought it was pretty self-explanatory. It's an old spy saying." She held up a hand. "*Not* that we're spies. Because we're not."

"Of course not. You just talk about them a lot."

"Actually, we do," Brad put in, a bit impatient to end this conversation. "Our culture celebrates those who work for justice and freedom, even if that work is carried out in secret. Now, let's drop the subject and talk about—"

He stopped abruptly and grabbed his sister's arm.

"What?" she asked irritably, pulling her arm away.

"Look." Brad nodded his head to indicate the appropriate direction.

Both she and Jacob turned to see what had gotten Brad's attention.

Moonlight filtering through the tall leafless trees faintly illuminated the forest floor. There was nothing unusual about that. And yet at some distance in the forest, the light was reflecting dully off of something.

"So?" Jacob asked, shrugging. "It's just fog. Although it doesn't seem to be the right kind of weather for fog…." His voice trailed off, as he realized the other two weren't really listening. He continued to look at the Everhearts, not understanding their reaction to the evening's weather.

"That's because… it's not just fog," Brad said. He looked at Kristen, who looked a little frightened.

He cleared his throat. "Yeah, listen, Jacob, we have to go," he said

"I thought we *were* going," the other boy replied, gesturing in the direction they'd been travelling.

"We were. But now have to go *this* way. Kris and I, that is."

"Into the fog?"

"Yes, into the fog."

"Is that where you're meeting your friends?"

"God, I hope so," Kristen muttered.

"Yes. Now listen," Brad said, turning his full attention to Jacob. "We have to go. You can't follow us. Whatever you do, do *not* walk into or toward that fog."

"But why would—"

"It doesn't matter. Just promise me."

Jacob clearly didn't understand why it was important that he not walk that way, in the direction of the fog, but apparently thought better of questioning it.

"Yes, I promise. I won't go near the fog."

"You'll go directly back to the tavern?" Brad pressed.

"Yes. If it's so important to you, then that's what I'll do. You have my word."

"Thank you. I know this sounds crazy and strange…."

"Well, it's been that kind of day," Jacob said, smiling ruefully.

"Yes. Yes, it has." Brad put his hand out. "You've been a good friend today, and I appreciate everything you've done for us."

Jacob shook his hand. "Actually, most of what I did, I did for Miss Darrow, at the request of Major Clark. You and Miss Everheart just happened to be with her. To tag along, so to speak."

"True, but still. Considering the role that Rebecca—Miss Darrow—played in these events today, and in the battle of White Marsh, it was important."

"The Battle of White Marsh? Is that what the attack will be called?"

Kristen spoke up. "Actually, thanks to her warning—or rather, the confirmation—it'll be less of an attack and more of a battle, since General Washington has been appropriately warned. And yes, it will be known as the Battle of White Marsh."

Jacob nodded and took Kristen's hand. He bowed over it and then kept hold of it slightly longer than necessary as he looked at her.

"Take care, Miss Everheart," he said.

He turned to start on his way—away from the fog—but then turned back. "I'm not going to see either of you again, am I?" he said, making it more of a statement than a question. "And you're really not from around here, are you?"

Brad smiled. "No, we're not."

"Then farewell to you both."

With a final wave, Jacob turned and disappeared once again into the trees.

Brad and Kristen were silent for a moment, looking at the point at which Jacob Tyson had melted into the forest. Then they looked at each other and turned toward the eerie mist.

"I'm almost afraid to do this," Kristen said. "What if it turns out to be just…fog?"

"Then we'll deal," Brad said firmly. "But being afraid is no reason not to try."

She nodded. "I'm ready."

*   *   *   *   *

They stepped toward the fog. Brad took his sister's hand and squeezed it reassuringly.

Perversely, like most fog, the farther the siblings advanced, the farther away the fog seemed to be. It was easy to see fog at a distance: up ahead, possibly, or behind; but not to be enveloped by it. Fog always seemed to be "over there," but never "right here."

Kristen didn't think they'd ever reach it, or at least, not reach it knowingly. It was possible, she'd observed, to never really be cognizant that you're really even in the fog. You never seem to 'enter' fog, she thought; you just seem to find it in front of you, or behind you, or off to the left and right.

This time was no exception. While the mystery mist still seemed to be ahead of them, Kristen noticed it was also around them, in every direction. It was almost as if she and Brad were in a bubble, a fog-free bubble, with the fog enveloping the outside of the bubble. They were "in" the fog, and yet the air for ten or twelve feet around them was clear.

"Are we in it?" she whispered. "Is this like the other fog?"

"I don't know. I didn't really pay attention last time. This morning it seemed like normal fog, and so does this one."

"This morning," Kristen repeated. "It seems like ages ago."

"Yeah, well, it wasn't. It's just about eight o'clock now, so it's barely been twelve hours."

She gave an unladylike snort. "More like a lifetime."

They continued on, each lost in thought.

"Wait," said Brad, stopping. "Is it me, or is the fog getting brighter?"

"Yeah, I guess it is. The moon's pretty bright, but even reflecting off the mist, it's not bright enough to make it look like this."

They continued ahead slowly.

"Maybe it's a good sign," Brad said, trying to sound positive. "Maybe it means this isn't just a normal fog."

He continued, and Kris could hear the humor in his voice. "Maybe this is the trademark of time-travel mist. You know, a gimmick, to distinguish itself from your normal, everyday, moisture-type fog."

She shook her head. "I think you have some sort of fog sickness, and you're getting a little stupid."

Now it was Kristen's turn to stop. "Wait! What if—"

"What?" he asked impatiently. "What if what?"

"What if this *is* special time-travel fog, but…. Well, what if it doesn't take us back where we started? What if it just takes us to some other time period altogether?"

"What in the world are you talking about?"

"Look, the fog brought us to this particular day in history, but what if it's not a direct, two-way connection? We have no guarantee it's going to take us back to our year... the exact same day and year that we left. I mean, what are the odds? When we walk out of that fog, we could find ourselves in this same physical spot, this same forest, in—literally—any day in history. 1492, 1650, 1927, or even the year 1000. Three-hundred and sixty-five days times two thousand years is… what, over seven-hundred thousand days? We could wind up in this godforsaken forest on any day for the past two thousand years."

Brad looked at her, and Kristen could see the flicker of doubt in his face. Doubt and worry.

"I hadn't thought of that. I just assumed— Doggone you, Kris! You picked a fine time to start thinking analytically. Not to mention being able to do math so quickly in your head."

He shook his head to clear it and looked annoyed.

"Look, technically, you right, I suppose it *is* possible we could wind up in some other day, some other year. But all that doesn't matter now. Right now, all that matters is that we have a choice: we either stay here, in *this* year, or we go through the fog. We have no reason to assume it will take us anywhere else. And unless you want to spend the rest of your life churning your own butter, sleeping on a straw mattress with fleas, and wearing clunky shoes that don't fit, I'd say our choice is clear."

Kristen looked at her brother for a moment, and then turned. "You're right. Let's go." To herself she muttered, "And let's just hope we don't end up in *The Land Before Time*."

As they continued into the fog, their steps slowed as the surrounding mist became brighter and brighter.

"Definitely not normal fog," Kristen noted.

After a few more steps, Brad stopped, his hand on his sister's arm.

"Listen! Do you hear that?"

"Hear what?"

"Shhh. Just listen."

She closed her eyes. "I don't hear-- Wait. Is that...."

"Traffic! I hear traffic on the highway."

"Oh, thank god—civilization! Mom and Dad must be killing themselves with worry."

"I know. Let's go!"

They began to jog, their packs slapping against their hips and sides. Kristen didn't care if she fell. She didn't care that she had torn the hem of her dress, or the fact that she hadn't eaten anything other than those Styrofoam-like journey cakes all day.

Brad felt the same. He'd done his best to be in charge and look after Kristen during this whole god-forsaken misadventure. He hadn't known what to do any more than she had, and he hadn't been any better equipped for what they'd faced. But because she was there, and she was younger than him, he'd done his best to bluff it out: to seem calm and logical and in control.

Truthfully, if it hadn't been for Kristen and the fact that he needed to be strong and confident for her sake, he wasn't sure how he would have handled this crazy experience.

Now, his main responsibility was to contact his parents as soon as possible so that whatever measures they had taken to find Kristen and him could be called to a halt.

As abruptly as it had appeared that morning... as quickly as things had spun out of control earlier... the surrounding mist suddenly disappeared.

And Kristen and Brad discovered why the fog had been so bright.

CHAPTER NINE

It was daylight.

Bright sun filtered through the trees.

Brad and Kristen blinked as they stood there, and looked around. Suddenly, there was no sign of the fog, behind them or anywhere else.

The dull hum of traffic was still audible in the distance, as well as the sound of a car door closing somewhere behind them.

The parking lot.

If they went back that way, they should find their car.

Right?

Brad reached into his bag and brought out his cellphone, flipping it on and thumbing a button.

"GPS! It knows where we are."

Kristen checked her phone too.

"No messages," she said, frowning. "That seems odd."

"And why is it light? Did the fog somehow transport us through the night and into the next day?"

"I don't know. But I find it hard to believe that nobody's left us any messages."

"I agree," Brad said. "Let's call mom and dad and tell them we're back. I'll bet they—"

Timekeepers: A Revolutionary Tale

Kristen grabbed his arm. "Someone's coming!" she whispered. "From up ahead."

"Why are you whispering?" her brother asked. "It's not like it's gonna be a British soldier and we have anything to hide."

No sooner had he said the words than they both saw it through the trees: a red coat advancing toward them.

Brad gasped. It couldn't be. They were back, they were home, in their own time. The sound of traffic confirmed that.

They *were* back... weren't they?

They heard a rustling behind them, and, turning, Brad saw someone approaching from the way he and Kristen had just come. He saw someone wearing buckskins and a brown coat and a slouch hat.

Jacob? Could Jacob had done what Brad had explicitly told him *not* to do, and followed them into the fog?

And the British soldier... he was advancing quickly; he would reach them first. Before Brad could react further, before he could grab Kristen's hand and run, the soldier was upon them.

The young man—tall, thin, dark hair, with black, narrow-rimmed glasses—nodded a greeting to the Everhearts and continued past them.

Meanwhile, the other person, the non-soldier, was coming up from behind.

Redcoat murmured a greeting and Buckskin returned it politely. Then Buckskin approached Brad and his sister.

"There you are," he said. "I wondered what had happened to you."

He looked at them from beneath the brim of his hat, and Brad's heart sank.

Jacob!

Kristen looked dismayed and confused too. "How did you—." She shook her head. "What are you doing here?"

The young man looked pointedly at her and then at Brad. "What am I doing here? The same thing you are, you idiots.

Extra credit in history class and the community service requirement, remember?"

He reached up and pulled off his hat, ruffling his hair as he did so.

Kristen and Brad looked at each other, comprehension flooding through them.

"Eric!" Brad said.

"Uh, yeah," Eric replied, and it came out with the clear implication of 'duh!' "It's me, in the flesh, you twits. What's up with you two? Why are you acting so weird?"

Brad shook his head as if to say 'if you only knew!'

"Sorry, dude," he said, as they continued walking. "We've had a rough day."

"Already? It's only eight o'clock. You can't have been up that long."

Kristen gave a snort. "You wouldn't think so, would you? And yet, it feels like we've already had a very full day."

Eric shook his head. "You look like it, too. Your dress is torn, at the bottom there, and you both look like you've been in a war."

He didn't see Kris and Brad exchange smiles.

"Hey, Eric," Kristen asked, "your family... they've lived in the area since colonial times, right?"

"Yeah, since the 1720s, I believe. My grandfather used to talk about our family moving to this area about then."

"And they owned a tavern?"

He looked at her. "So the story goes. Why? How do you know about that?"

Kris shrugged. "Just a little tidbit I picked up in some research."

"Research? What are you researching? And why?"

"Oh, just learning a little more about the Battle of White Marsh. Or rather, what led up to it."

Eric laughed as they walked down the dirt path. "There was a war going on, and two armies faced off against each other, right in this very spot. That's what led up to it."

Timekeepers: A Revolutionary Tale

"Do you have any idea if your ancestors fought in the war? Or played any part in it at all?"

Eric frowned as he thought about it. Kristen had already thought he was cute: dark hair, blue eyes framed by dark lashes, great cheekbones. She felt that Jacob had been equally good-looking, although his hair had been lighter, more dirty-blond than anything.

But she could see some of Jacob in Eric.

In answer to her question, he said, "I don't know that I've ever heard of my ancestors fighting in the war. They may have, though. But they definitely owned the tavern at that time."

Brad turned to look at his classmate. "Even if they weren't soldiers, that doesn't mean they weren't involved in the war," he said. "I mean, think about it: what better way to serve your country than to operate a tavern, where people congregate and stop in as they travel from one place to another. It'd be a great way to gather information."

Eric stopped.

"Wait," he said, and the others stopped too. "Are you saying… are you implying that my great-great-however-many-greats-grandfather… could have been a spy?"

"Not really a spy," said Kristen. "Just—er, well—in the intelligence business. For our side, of course," she added hastily.

Eric looked from one sibling to the other.

"Cool!" he said. "I could totally see that happening."

The three continued walking, but Kristen dropped back next to Brad.

"Listen, when we get home later, think you could show me some of the info you got on Rebecca's mom?"

"Lydia Darragh? Sure, but there isn't much. Her story is anecdotal and was never able to be completely verified."

"That's okay; just whatever you were able to find." She didn't say it out loud, but Kristen knew that, if it was out there,

Brad would have found it in his research, and anything he hadn't found probably wasn't worth knowing.

"What are you going to do with the information?" he asked.

"I thought I'd put it in my report for the community service requirement. It's a great story, and we know it's true, so maybe more people should know about it."

"Y'know, I wonder…" Brad said.

"What?"

"I wonder if maybe there is something out there about Jacob's family. You know, the tavern, the intelligence-gathering, and the role his family played in the war."

"I would think there'd have to be something… somewhere."

He shook his head. "I don't know. I researched the whole thing pretty thoroughly—everything that led to the Battle of White Marsh. I think I would have noticed or remembered something that mentioned the name Tyson."

"Maybe it was never made public. Maybe it was kept in the family. Who knows, maybe Eric's family has something about it—old letters or a journal or something."

"Could be."

"Or—" Kristen said as a thought struck her, "what about Major Clark? I bet there's a record of him somewhere. I mean, he was a military man, after all."

"You're right, I bet there is. Good thinking." He put out his hand for a fist bump.

"You know, it's funny," Kristen said. "Everybody thinks that where they live is so boring: nothing going on, nothing ever happens, that sort of thing. But even if you live in a small town, chances are there's a lot more interesting stuff and history than you realize, and all you have to do is look for it."

"Yeah, I guess that's a lesson learned. And you know, that may have been the whole point of this… adventure. Otherwise, why us? Why were *we* sent—today, the day of a battle re-enactment—back to the exact point at which the scales were tipped in the favor of the Continentals?"

When she raised her eyebrows, he continued. "You said it yourself to Jacob: if Rebecca hadn't delivered her message, it would have been more of an attack than a battle, and the Americans would probably have lost. The heavy defeat, the oncoming winter, the soldiers not being paid... our army would have been demoralized, there would have been desertions by the dozen, and who knows what consequences there would have been."

"Instead, Washington was made aware of details of the attack, and kicked some redcoat butt."

"Right. Even small victories can have major repercussions. So the question remains: why us, and why today?"

Kristen shrugged. "Maybe this story needs telling."

"May be. Maybe there are a lot of stories of small actions that have big consequences. And maybe those stories need to be told, too."

"But the next question is: if someone tells one of these stories, will anyone believe it? After all, it's just a 'story;' there is no actual proof."

It was Brad's turn to shrug. "Well, maybe it all depends on how the story is told. A community service report, a research paper—who knows, maybe even a novel."

Kristen smiled. "Yeah, I hear that. Mom has always said she learned more from historical novels than she ever did in history class."

"And there's plenty of it out there. As you said a minute ago: whether it's history in general, or the history of some small town, or an obscure battle... all you have to do is look for it, and chances are, you'll find something pretty darned cool."

Kristen's cell phone rang, and she reached into her backpack to answer it, once again looking forward to the "normal" Saturday activities that she so recently had been lamenting.

In a similar frame of mind, Brad called out to his friend.

"Yo, Eric! Wait up…."

The End

Timekeepers: A Revolutionary Tale

Author's Note:

I hope you enjoyed *Timekeepers: A Revolutionary Tale.* It was fun to write—and fun to read about the history surrounding these events.

The Battle of White Marsh was real. It wasn't a big battle, but it was important nonetheless. However, as an author I took a minor liberty in the timeline. This book places the battle in the autumn, when the actual event took place in December, 1777. I know, most of December technically is in autumn, but I didn't want to use the 'real' date as that would have the two teenagers roaming around the Pennsylvania forest in one of the coldest months of the year.

The story of Lydia Darragh is also real. As told here, it's not well documented and not officially confirmed, but the tale exists. Once again, I took a few liberties for the sake of good storytelling, but the basis of the "spy" story is true.

If you enjoyed *A Revolutionary Tale*, you might also enjoy more of the Everhearts' *Timekeepers* adventures. In *Civil Disturbance*, Brad and Kristen find themselves flung back to the nineteenth century, at the tail end of one monumental event and at the cusp of another... and this time, they each travel back in time separately. Additionally, in *Good as Gold*, the siblings have a hand in events relating to the first gold discovered in North America. Finally, the most recent Timekeepers book, *Computer Zero,* tells a little about the creation of, well, the first computer.

Timekeepers: A Revolutionary Tale - set during the American Revolution

Timekeepers: Civil Disturbance – takes place at the tail end of the Civil War

Timekeepers: Good as Gold – early 1800s, first discovery of gold in North America

J. Y. Harris

Timekeepers: Computer Zero – set in the early 1940s…
and you know what was happening *then*

I'd love to hear your opinion of the Timekeepers books.
please take a moment to leave a review on the site where you
purchased the book.   Or, feel free to e-mail me at
jyharrisbooks@gmail.com, or visit the J.Y. Harris Books page
on Facebook.

Thanks for letting me tell my story. Keep reading!

Made in the USA
Columbia, SC
13 January 2019